ANIMAL
Stories

Favourite
ANIMAL
Stories

chosen by

RED FOX

A Red Fox Book

Published by Random House Children's Books
20 Vauxhall Bridge Road, London SW1V 2SA

A division of The Random House Group Ltd
London Melbourne Sydney Auckland
Johannesburg and agencies throughout the world

3 5 7 9 10 8 6 4 2

First published by The Bodley Head Children's Books 2000

This edition 2001

Printed and bound in Great Britain by
Bookmarque Ltd, Croydon, Surrey

Papers used by The Random House Group Limited are natural,
recyclable products made from wood grown in sustainable forest.
The manufacturing processes conform to the environmental
regulations of the country of origin.

The Random House Group Limited Reg. No. 954009

www.randomhouse.co.uk

ISBN 0 09 941343 4

Contents

Introduction

For my seventh birthday I was given a book called *The Magic Pudding*. What an unlikely title for something that would literally change my life! I guess my parents bought it for me initially because it had superb illustrations, all drawn by the author, Norman Lindsay. They were very keen to encourage my interest in drawing, and Lindsay was an established Australian artist. His mastery of pencil, pen and brush, both in oils and water colour, and his superb etching technique had already made him a legend in the art world, when he suddenly decided to turn his attention to drawing and writing for children.

The way this came about was quite interesting. Lindsay was lunching with a very important publisher, and the subject of children's books prompted Lindsay to say that he thought European fairy stories didn't really interest Australian kids. They were much more interested in food, he claimed, than in elves, goblins or pixies. "Pick any food," he continued, "and I'll write you a best seller about it that'll beat fairy stories hands down." "Bet you can't write a book about a pudding," laughed the publisher. Lindsay took on the bet, and in a short time he'd written a very Australian book, illustrated on almost every page with the most wonderful pictures. It was a runaway best seller and he won his bet! This book opened up a whole new world for me. I just loved the colourful Aussie language, with its comic inventive slang, and I read it over and over again. Even now, some sixty odd years later, I can quote you almost any page and I'm still word perfect!

As a direct result of the joy I experienced with the Puddin', I began to read every other book I could lay my hands on. I had loved A. A. Milne's books when my mum read them to me, and *The Wind in the Willows* naturally followed, with its glimpse of an ordered English way of life that was completely different to what I was used to in Perth, Western Australia. I could NOT stop reading and, happily, my parents kept making books available to me as and when they could afford them. I raced through *Black Beauty*, *The Call of the Wild*, *The Jungle Book*, and many Australian books that are sadly now out of print. I vividly remember the gradual transition from books like *The Magic Pudding,* with its many illustrations, to books with maybe an illustration at the start of each chapter, and eventually to books with no illustrations at all. At first I really missed the pictures, but after a while I realised that my imagination painted better pictures than anyone else could possibly create.

I've put together a selection of extracts from my favourite childhood stories that involve animals, and the publishers have commissioned some others. I hope this book, with a few of my illustrations dotted about, will encourage you to become as hooked on reading as I have been.

I, Houdini

by Lynne Reid Banks

Houdini the hamster has one aim in life – to escape. His adventures take him all over the house; inside the piano, under floorboards and even up the chimney, leaving a trail of destruction behind him. But he is about to develop a whole new idea of what freedom means...

Oh, it was wonderful to be free! I scampered down those steps in a twinkling. A feeling of almost hysterical delight came over me as I saw that all the doors downstairs were open. Lights were out – everyone had gone to bed – but it wasn't too dark to see my way, and there were plenty of smells to guide me. I headed for the living-room first, the piano-room I call it. I was so overjoyed to get back into my piano again! I hadn't realised till then that I had grown – I was now full-size – and to my excitement I found I could now climb right to the top inside. There was a marvellous place there, with rows of little wooden hammer-things with their tips covered in lovely soft felt. Ah, I thought. Perfect for a nest! I'd already planned, during my weeks of imprisonment, how I would make nests all over the house to retreat to if I ever got the chance, and stock them with food so that no matter what room I was in I would have a safe refuge where I could stay for some days.

I got to work on the felts. As soon as I had chewed off enough soft stuff to fill both cheeks I would nip down to a platform I had found about halfway to the ground, de-cheek the bedding, and then climb up to get more. I did the better part of the whole nest before I allowed myself time off to forage for a bite to eat.

I thought I'd have to go to the kitchen for that, but there was a really delicious smell right there in the living-room which I decided to investigate first. I traced it to the area of the fireplace. It was coming down from above somewhere – a fresh, fruity smell, richer and moister than grain. I determined to find out what it was, and get some, if it was any good. But how to get up there?

After several head-on attempts which the still-glowing embers foiled, I went to the side of the fireplace. There I found a perfect way up. Mind you I won't say it was easy. It was a straight wall, with a sticking-out bit covered with rough stuff like brick or cement; but the wall, luckily for me, was covered with some material like sacking. This gave me all the foothold I needed and, feet spread, I was up that angle as quickly as I went up my tubes at home. Pretty soon I was on the mantelpiece above the fire, and there I found my prize.

It was a large vase full of sprays of red berries. I'd never tasted a berry before, but I had had fresh fruit and salad so I knew it would be good. I scrambled up the wall, pressing my back against the vase, and pretty soon I was having a marvellous time swinging on the sturdy branches and twigs, scoffing these little red berries until neither my stomach nor my cheeks could hold any more.

I was just turning my thoughts – not without some worries – to the much more difficult downward climb, when I spotted a particularly luscious looking bunch of berries right out on the tip of the branch I was on. Yes, it was sheer greed that made me go for them – I don't deny it. I just couldn't bear to leave them there. Also, perhaps my antics in the piano and on the stairs had made me too confident. None too cautiously I began to edge along the branch towards the cluster...

Need I go on? With the added weight of the berries in my cheeks, I was too heavy. The branch, the berries, the vase and I were all soon lying in a puddle of water in the hearth, the air around still echoing with the crash

11

the vase made as it broke.

Well, I thought, picking myself up with a dainty shake of my wet fur, at least that solves the problem of getting down. But there was another problem now, because the noise had woken the Father, who could already be heard thumping about upstairs. Houdini, said I to myself, this is no place for you! Quick as thought, I scurried behind the piano and up into my brand-new nest.

The rows about the telephone wire and the carpet and the door were as nothing compared to what followed my escapade on the mantelpiece. The Father seemed to go completely mad. He literally jumped up and down, purple in the face with rage. (How do I know? I'll tell you. There was a little window in my piano – actually a little sliding-glass panel. Don't ask me why, but it was extremely useful, as I could sit on the hammers in a shadow and peep out at what was going on in the living-room. That was where the light came from, inside.) He did more than threaten now – he issued ultimatums. "No more chances!" he bellowed. "Back it goes! That, or I'll kill it – I will – I'll kill it with my bare hands!"

Yes, very intemperate of him, wasn't it? And all that was before he'd discovered – what needless to say I had not known – that all that soft stuff I chewed off the little wooden hammers prevented a number of notes from playing on the piano.

He went to the lengths of pulling the piano out from the wall, taking its back off, and hunting for me through all the works. My nest was demolished, of course, and my store of berries was stolen. But fortunately for me, by that time I was no longer there. I had found my favourite place under the kitchen floor.

⚙

My luck seemed to be in altogether, so far as that kitchen was concerned.

It was not one of your shining modern affairs with all the gadgets, stoves, washing-machines and so forth set so tightly side by side that even a mouse couldn't squeeze between them – no. It was your old-fashioned, half-converted kind, with huge chasms between and behind the bits of equipment. I could safely run right under the stove, for instance, and one of the cabinets – the one which turned out to contain my beloved biscuit drawer – had no back. The drawer itself, three shelves up, was not quite backless, but its back was half broken so that, having swung up to it, it was a simple matter to climb in and help myself. The children's visits to that drawer left it in such chaos that it was a long time before the Mother realised that most of the crumbs, torn wrappings etc., were my work.

Well! So on my very first exploration of this domestic paradise I discovered, in one corner under the sink, a hole in the floor. You may imagine I was exceedingly careful not to go down into it until I had checked on the distance of the drop below, but I soon realised that there was a sort of handy little platform just there, with the real floor about five inches underneath. The platform had been built to hide a strange tangle of pipes of various kinds which snaked about in the dark under the false floor. They didn't bother me, however. I soon learnt which ones were hot and which weren't, and in fact they provided several

13

cosy little nooks and crannies, in one of which I decided to build my permanent home.

It took labour and planning of course – what dream house doesn't? I lost count of the number of trips I made in the dead of night, carrying all kinds of lovely soft bedding material – carpet fluff, shavings, bits of chewed-up fabrics which I found carelessly left lying about (how could I know that useless-looking stripy-thing was Mark's school tie?) Anyway, by the time I had arranged everything to my satisfaction a number of days had passed and I'm afraid the family had begun to despair of ever seeing me again, because I was very careful to work only after they had gone to bed in order not to draw attention to my activities.

Nobody, I was determined, was going to find this nest – it was the most beautiful I had ever constructed. Nowhere, not even the piano, had I felt so safe and warm and comfortable. The first night I bedded down there, after feasting from a splendid supply of grain, crumbs and (treat of treats!) raisins that I had found readily available, I felt utterly contented and pleased with myself.

There was just one thing that was not quite perfect. My under-floor home lacked a built-in water supply.

When I got thirsty I had to go out and forage for drink. Sometimes there would be a puddle of water left on the floor near the sink, but I felt lapping up spilt water – often tasting disgustingly of detergent – was beneath my dignity.

The surest source was, of course, my own water bottle in the cage, but that meant going all the way upstairs, slithering back into the opening I had made, having a drink and rushing home again. I could never climb in or out of the cage without making some noise, and I paid for every drink I took in this way in sheer terror that one of the boys would hear me and come out and capture me.

The infuriating thing was, there *was* water under the platform. In fact I came to realise that one of the pipes which surrounded my nest was a water-pipe. I knew this because there was a joint further along, out of which, when the pressure was high, a few drops of water sometimes leaked. Each time this happened I would think, "How marvellous if there were a tiny hole in the pipe through which I could suck a drink whenever I wanted one!"

This thought preyed on my mind. I would often lie in bed (as you would put it), with comforting rays of light filtering through the cracks in the floorboards, and gaze at that pipe, almost willing it to spring a leak. Needless to say it didn't, but eventually, one hot night when my thirst was tormenting me and I just didn't feel like climbing mountains and running risks to get water, I decided to do something about it.

I had long ago learnt that gnawing on metal is useless and painful. That was why I had not had a go at that pipe before. But what I now discovered was that not all metals are alike. I thought they were all equally hard and resistant. But as soon as I tried an experimental gnaw, I found that this kind was – well, not soft, of course not, but certainly no harder than a lot of woods.

In fact I must say that gnawing on this stuff was really very satisfying. If I didn't try to bite it, but just applied my side-teeth to peeling off little threads of it, it came away beautifully. It also wore my teeth down beautifully, so that the process of actually making a hole in the thing took over a week. I didn't want to find myself with stubs instead of teeth.

I made my breakthrough on a Saturday night. I know that because the family usually lie in late on a Sunday, enabling me to be out and about in the morning after my usual bedtime, foraging for special tidbits for my own Sunday lunch.

On this occasion, though, there was no Sunday lunch for anybody.

At dawn, after a night's work, I sensed that I was about to pierce the water-pipe. I was belly-deep in fine lead shavings. There was a long shallow channel of bright, shining metal where I was working, grooved with my toothmarks. I must be nearly there! I could feel the extra coldness of water, right against my lips as I worked. Just one more good gnaw —

Whoosh!

The next second I was flat on my back. A jet of water, which had hit me in the face and bowled me over, was making a swift-running stream across the floor. My lovely nest was awash, my fur soaked. I jumped up and fled into a far corner, out of the way of the stream, which rapidly enlarged into a river. The water as it came out of the pipe made a hissing noise every bit as sinister as the hiss of an enraged hamster. For my part, I was dumb with horror. What, oh what had I done?

I had certainly blown my hiding place and my home, that was sure. I decided that discretion, as they say, was the better part of valour. I waded across the

16

river, which was now flowing out from under the platform over the rest of the kitchen floor, came up through my entrance hole, took one appalled look at the spreading lake, and ran as fast as my little legs would carry me to the safest place I could think of. My cage. Foolishly no doubt, I thought that if I were found there, a self-surrendered captive, suspicion would not fall on me.

I cowered in my loft, wondering what was happening downstairs and willing someone to go down and stop the water before the whole house was flooded. At the same time I hoped they never would, for I could not imagine what sort of row would follow. Perhaps I wouldn't be blamed? I had all too little hope. The Father had become quite neurotic about me, blaming me for everything that went wrong in the house, including the loss of his hammer and the disappearance (later traced to Guy) of a two-pound box of after-dinner mints. As if I'd be caught dead eating anything so bad for my teeth! (Well, except on festive occasions!)

At last Mark got up and padded sleepily downstairs to get something to eat. I crouched with closed eyes, every nerve alert for the outcry. It came, shatteringly.

"MUMMY! DADDY! The kitchen's flooded!"

A moment later he came flying up the stairs, his face alight with excitement and delight. I cowered down in the musty old bedding I hadn't used for weeks. The loft roof overhead was clear, and as the Mother and Father, roused from their Sunday lie-in, came pelting along the corridor I felt as if the ceiling were about to fall on me. What a fool I'd been to go to my cage! What a simpleton!

The whole family thundered past me and down the stairs like a herd of elephants, and I crouched, waiting for the explosion. Of course you'll say I should have wriggled out and fled to a secure hiding place straight away, but the shameful truth was I was too terrified to move. I heard the Father give voice to a bellow of dismay, while everyone else uttered shrieks and cries and exclamations and questions that went on for about ten minutes, seemed like ten hours to me. I expected every second that they would come thundering up again and rend me limb from limb. But to my great relief, nothing of the sort happened.

Slowly everything quietened down. After a bit the boys were sent upstairs to dry their feet (I assume they'd all been paddling) and get dressed. As Adam went past the cage he suddenly stopped dead.

"Look!" he cried in wonder. "It's Houdini! He's back!"

I opened one eye just long enough to see they were all crouching round me, and then I pretended to be asleep. There was such a long silence, though, that I had another peep to see why they weren't talking. The reason was, they were all looking at each other and then at me. When they did speak, it was in whispers.

"Why would he go back in by himself?"

"Unless he had a guilty conscience!"

"What's that?" hissed Guy. (It was the first time I'd heard the expression, but I knew what it meant all right!)

"He knows he did something awful, Dumbo!" Mark hissed back. "And we know what it was!"

"But we mustn't tell!" Adam said, forgetting to

whisper. Mark bowled him over backwards and sat on his head.

"SHHHH! If Dad ever finds out it was him…"

"If we guessed, he will too!" croaked Adam from underneath Mark.

"Then we'll take Houdini out of there and hide him somewhere else till the trouble blows over."

And that, friends, is how I found myself back in that thrice-accursed bin.

With the lid on.

❧

While it was very comforting to feel that the children were on my side, it was horrible to be incarcerated in that bin, even though I had richly deserved it. I had to stay there for nearly two whole days. They fed me of course, and let me out for a run at night after the lights were supposed to be out, but that didn't really help. To make matters worse, I lived in dread of discovery, especially after I heard Mark say, on the Monday morning:

"The plumber's coming. Daddy's taking the floorboards up."

'Daddy' was nobody's fool. I knew the minute he saw the marks of my teeth on that pipe, I was as good as done for.

The bellow he had made when he first saw the flood was but a faint whimper compared to the roar he let out when the boards came up and my crime was revealed.

"THAT ANIMAL! That – that – that little misbegotten son of a verminous flea-bitten cross-eyed sewer-rat! Wait till I lay my hands on him – just wait…"

I lost my head at this point and began running round and round inside the bin in an agony of terror. Mark heard me and lifted the lid long enough to whisper: "Keep still, you idiot! If he comes up here he'll hear you!"

Then he put the lid back and he and his brothers seemed to be dropping all sorts of stuff on top and around the bin to hide it. I lay in the suffocating darkness and wondered whether the Father really meant even half the things he was threatening to do when he caught up with me.

·Mercifully I never found out. (Incidentally I'm prepared to give him the benefit of the doubt. He's not a bad sort really, he's just got this fearful temper.) When Mark came home from school that afternoon, following a day which I would prefer to forget entirely, he had a master-plan.

I was to be lent to a neighbour, cage and all, for as long as it took the Father to calm down. I heard the boys discussing it. This neighbour also had a hamster, it seemed, so I would not be lonely. Personally I didn't care for any company whatever just then, but never mind. It would be a huge relief just to be out of the house and safe from the Father's righteous wrath.

In any case, even this disaster had not completely dampened my love of change and adventure. I had pretty well exhausted the possibilities of my own family's house – I certainly had no objections to exploring another.

So, when the Father and Mother were closeted before the television, Adam popped me back in my cage and he and Mark crept downstairs, holding it between them, with Guy bringing up the rear with my bag of feed. Out of the doors we went, and I had my first glimpse of the great big world of the street outside.

It was a revelation, of course. The size of it – the scope! I had had no idea, till that moment, that there was a world outside houses. Well – I suppose I had known, from pictures and telly and so on, that an Outdoors existed. But the moment I saw it, smelt it, I knew I could not rest until I had escaped from Indoors and explored the wonderful, vast, fresh-scented world of under-the-sky.

Esio Trot

by Roald Dahl

*Mr Hoppy lives in the flat above Mrs Silver. For
many years he has watched her from his balcony and
he is in love with her, but is too shy to let her know. He
is desperate to do something that will win her heart,
but he has a rival for her affections – a small tortoise,
called Alfie…*

Alfie had been with Mrs Silver for years and he lived
on her balcony summer and winter. Planks had been
placed around the sides of the balcony so that Alfie
could walk about without toppling over the edge, and
in one corner there was a little house into which Alfie
would crawl every night to keep warm.

When the colder weather came along in November,
Mrs Silver would fill Alfie's house with dry hay, and the
tortoise would crawl in there and bury himself deep
under the hay and go to sleep for months on end
without food or water. This is called hibernating.

In early spring, when Alfie felt the warmer weather
through his shell, he would wake up and crawl very
slowly out of his house on to the balcony. And Mrs

Silver would clap her hands with joy and cry out, "Welcome back, my darling one! Oh, how I have missed you!"

It was at times like these that Mr Hoppy wished more than ever that he could change places with Alfie and become a tortoise.

Now we come to a certain bright morning in May when something happened that changed and indeed electrified Mr Hoppy's life. He was leaning over his balcony-rail watching Mrs Silver serving Alfie his breakfast.

"Here's the heart of the lettuce for you, my lovely," she was saying. "And here's a slice of fresh tomato and a piece of crispy celery."

"Good morning, Mrs Silver," Mr Hoppy said. "Alfie's looking well this morning."

"Isn't he gorgeous!" Mrs Silver said, looking up and beaming at him.

"Absolutely gorgeous," Mr Hoppy said, not meaning it. And now, as he looked down at Mrs Silver's smiling face gazing up into his own, he thought for the thousandth time how pretty she was, how sweet and gentle and full of kindness, and his heart ached with love.

"I do so wish he would *grow* a little faster," Mrs Silver was saying. "Every spring, when he wakes up from his winter sleep, I weigh him on the kitchen scales. And do you know that in all the eleven years I've had him he's not gained more than *three ounces*! That's almost *nothing*!"

"What does he weigh now?" Mr Hoppy asked her.

"Just thirteen ounces," Mrs Silver answered. "About

23

as much as a grapefruit."

"Yes, well, tortoises are very slow growers," Mr Hoppy said solemnly. "But they can live for a hundred years."

"I know that," Mrs Silver said. "But I do so wish he would grow just a little bit bigger. He's such a tiny wee fellow."

"He seems just fine as he is," Mr Hoppy said.

"No, he's *not* just fine!" Mrs Silver cried. "Try to think how miserable it must make him feel to be so titchy! Everyone wants to grow up."

"You really *would* love him to grow bigger, wouldn't you?" Mr Hoppy said, and even as he said it his mind suddenly went *click* and an amazing idea came rushing into his head.

"Of course I would!" Mrs Silver cried. "I'd give *anything* to make it happen! Why, I've seen pictures of giant tortoises that are so huge people can ride on their backs! If Alfie were to see those he'd turn green with envy!"

Mr Hoppy's mind was spinning like a flywheel. Here, surely, was his big chance! Grab it, he told himself. Grab it quick!

"Mrs Silver," he said. "I do actually happen to know how to make tortoises grow faster, if that's really what you want."

"You do?" she cried. "Oh, please tell me! Am I feeding him the wrong things?"

"I worked in North Africa once," Mr Hoppy said. "That's where all these tortoises in England come from, and a Bedouin tribesman told me the secret."

"Tell me!" cried Mrs Silver. "I beg you to tell me, Mr

Hoppy! I'll be your slave for life."

When he heard the words *your slave for life*, a little shiver of excitement swept through Mr Hoppy. "Wait there," he said. "I'll have to go in and write something down for you."

In a couple of minutes Mr Hoppy was back on the balcony with a sheet of paper in his hand. "I'm going to lower it to you on a bit of string," he said, "or it might blow away. Here it comes."

Mrs Silver caught the paper and held it up in front of her. This is what she read:

ESIO TROT, ESIO TROT,
TEG REGGIB REGGIB!
EMOC NO, ESIO TROT,
WORG PU, FFUP PU, TOOHS PU!
GNIRPS PU, WOLB PU, LLEWS PU!
EGROG! ELZZUG! FFUTS! PLUG!
TUP NO TAF, ESIO TROT, TUP NO TAF!
TEG NO, TEG NO! ELBBOG DOOF!

"What *does* it mean?" she asked. "Is it another language?"

"It's tortoise language," Mr Hoppy said. "Tortoises are very backward creatures. Therefore they can only understand words that are written backwards. That's obvious, isn't it?"

"I suppose so," Mrs Silver said, bewildered.

"Esio trot is simply tortoise spelled backwards," Mr Hoppy said. "Look at it."

"So it is," Mrs Silver said.

"The other words are spelled backwards, too," Mr

Hoppy said. "If you turn them round into human language, they simply say:

TORTOISE, TORTOISE,
GET BIGGER BIGGER!
COME ON, TORTOISE,
GROW UP, PUFF UP, SHOOT UP!
SPRING UP, BLOW UP, SWELL UP!
GORGE! GUZZLE! STUFF! GULP!
PUT ON FAT, TORTOISE, PUT ON FAT!
GET ON, GET ON! GOBBLE FOOD!"

Mrs Silver examined the magic words on the paper more closely. "I guess you're right," she said. "How clever. But there's an awful lot of poos in it. Are they something special?"

"Poo is a very strong word in any language," Mr Hoppy said, "especially with tortoises. Now what you have to do, Mrs Silver, is hold Alfie up to your face and whisper these words to him three times a day, morning, noon and night. Let me hear you practise them."

Very slowly and stumbling a little over the strange words, Mrs Silver read the whole message out loud in tortoise language.

"Not bad," Mr Hoppy said. "But try to get a little more expression into it when you say it to Alfie. If you do it properly I'll bet you anything you like that in a few months' time he'll be twice as big as he is now."

"I'll try it," Mrs Silver said. "I'll try anything. Of course I will. But I can't believe it'll work."

"You wait and see," Mr Hoppy said, smiling at her.

Back in his flat, Mr Hoppy was simply quivering all

over with excitement. *Your slave for life*, he kept repeating to himself. What bliss!

But there was a lot of work to be done before that happened.

The only furniture in Mr Hoppy's small living-room was a table and two chairs. These he moved into his bedroom. Then he went out and bought a sheet of thick canvas and spread it over the entire living-room floor to protect his carpet.

Next, he got out the telephone-book and wrote down the address of every pet-shop in the city. There were fourteen of them altogether.

It took him two days to visit each pet-shop and choose his tortoises. He wanted a great many, at least one hundred, perhaps more. And he had to choose them very carefully.

To you and me there is not much difference between one tortoise and another. They differ only in their size and in the colour of their shells. Alfie had a darkish shell, so Mr Hoppy chose only the darker-shelled tortoises for his great collection.

Size, of course, was everything. Mr Hoppy chose all sorts of different sizes, some weighing only slightly more than Alfie's thirteen ounces, others a great deal more, but he didn't want any that weighed less.

"Feed them cabbage leaves," the pet-shop owners told him. "That's all they'll need. And a bowl of water."

When he had finished, Mr Hoppy, in his enthusiasm, had bought no less than one hundred and forty tortoises and he carried them home in baskets, ten or fifteen at a time. He had to make a lot of trips and he was quite exhausted at the end of it all, but it was worth it. Boy, was it worth it! And what an amazing sight his living-room was when they were all in there together! The floor was swarming with tortoises of different sizes, some walking slowly about and exploring, some munching cabbage leaves, others drinking water from a big shallow dish. They made just the faintest rustling sound as they moved over the canvas sheet, but that was all. Mr Hoppy had to pick his way carefully on his toes between this moving sea of brown shells whenever he walked across the room. But enough of that. He must get on with the job.

Before he retired Mr Hoppy had been a mechanic in a bus-garage. And now he went back to his old place of work and asked his mates if he might use his old bench for an hour or two.

What he had to do now was to make something that would reach down from his own balcony to Mrs Silver's balcony and pick up a tortoise. This was not difficult for a mechanic like Mr Hoppy.

First he made two metal claws or fingers, and these he attached to the end of a long metal tube. He ran two stiff wires down inside the tube and connected them to the metal claws in such a way that when you pulled the wires, the claws closed, and when you pushed them, the claws opened. The wires were joined to a handle at the other end of the tube. It was all very simple.

Mr Hoppy was ready to begin.

Mrs Silver had a part-time job. She worked from noon until five o'clock every weekday afternoon in a shop that sold newspapers and sweets. That made things a lot easier for Mr Hoppy.

So on that first exciting afternoon, after he had

made sure that Mrs Silver had gone to work, Mr Hoppy went out on to his balcony armed with his long metal pole. He called this his tortoise-catcher. He leaned over the balcony railings and lowered the pole down on to Mrs Silver's balcony below. Alfie was basking in the pale sunlight over to one side.

"Hello Alfie," Mr Hoppy said. "You are about to go for a little ride."

He wiggled the tortoise-catcher till it was right above Alfie. He pushed the hand-lever so that the claws opened wide. Then he lowered the two claws neatly over Alfie's shell and pulled the lever. The claws closed tightly over the shell like two fingers of a hand. He hauled Alfie up on to his own balcony. It was easy.

Mr Hoppy weighed Alfie on his own kitchen scales just to make sure that Mrs Silver's figure of thirteen ounces was correct. It was.

Now, holding Alfie in one hand, he picked his way carefully through his huge collection of tortoises to find one that first of all had the same colour shell as Alfie's and secondly weighed *exactly two ounces more*.

Two ounces is not much. It is less than a smallish hen's egg weighs. But you see, the important thing in Mr Hoppy's plan was to make sure that the new tortoise was bigger than Alfie but only a *tiny bit* bigger. The difference had to be so small that Mrs Silver wouldn't notice it.

From his vast collection, it was not difficult for Mr Hoppy to find just the tortoise he wanted. He wanted one that weighed fifteen ounces exactly on his kitchen scales, no more and no less. When he had got it, he put it on the kitchen table beside Alfie, and even he could hardly tell that one was bigger than the other. But it *was* bigger. It was bigger by two ounces. This was Tortoise Number 2.

Mr Hoppy took Tortoise Number 2 out on to the balcony and gripped it in the claws of his tortoise-catcher. Then he lowered it on to Mrs Silver's balcony, right beside a nice fresh lettuce leaf.

Tortoise Number 2 had never eaten tender juicy lettuce leaves before. It had only had thick old cabbage leaves. It loved the lettuce and started chomping away at it with great gusto.

There followed a rather nervous two hours' wait for Mrs Silver to return from work.

Would she see any difference between the new

30

tortoise and Alfie? It was going to be a tense moment.

Out on to her balcony swept Mrs Silver.

"Alfie, my darling!" she cried out. "Mummy's back! Have you missed me?"

Mr Hoppy, peering over his railing, but well hidden between two huge potted plants, held his breath.

The new tortoise was still chomping away at the lettuce.

"My my, Alfie, you do seem hungry today," Mrs Silver was saying. "It must be Mr Hoppy's magic words I've been whispering to you."

Mr Hoppy watched as Mrs Silver picked the tortoise up and stroked his shell. Then she fished Mr Hoppy's piece of paper out of her pocket, and holding the tortoise very close to her face, she whispered, reading from the paper:

"ESIO TROT, ESIO TROT,
TEG REGGIB REGGIB!
EMOC NO, ESIO TROT,
WORG PU, FFUP PU, TOOHS PU!
GNIRPS PU, WOLB PU, LLEWS PU!
EGROG! ELZZUG! FFUTS! PLUG!
TUP NO TAF, ESIO TROT, TUP NO TAF!
TEG NO, TEG NO! ELBBOG DOOF!"

Mr Hoppy popped his head out of the foliage and called out, "Good evening, Mrs Silver. How is Alfie tonight?"

"Oh, he's lovely," Mrs Silver said, looking up

and beaming. "And he's developing such an appetite! I've never seen him eat like this before! It must be the magic words."

"You never know," Mr Hoppy said darkly. "You never know."

Stella

by Adèle Geras

The cat who hangs around my local library has magic powers. I won't tell you which library it is: they wouldn't appreciate being hassled by curious visitors, and Stella would probably run away. She's the cat. Her real home is in the off-licence next door (they call her Stella after the lager), but it didn't take her long to work out that libraries have soft carpets, and off-licences do not. Libraries are visited by children who stop and stroke her. They have warm radiators to stretch out on... etc., etc.

To look at her, you'd never guess that she was in any way special. She's a skinny little thing, not much bigger than a big kitten, and her coat is mostly white, with some black blotches scattered about. She used to sit in the reference library most of the time, where there are armchairs she can curl up on if nobody else is sitting on them.

And then the library went online. Five computers were moved into the entrance hall, and the catalogue was no longer to be found in wooden boxes full of index cards. As soon as word got round that you could surf the net for nothing in the library, everyone began to use the computers, including my Auntie Trixie. She's the reason I know about the magic powers. Stella worked her magic with my aunt. This is how it happened.

Aunt Trixie loved the library. She used to go in there for books, for warmth, for chat, and when they started getting CDs and videos, she was delighted. Then the computers came, and Aunt Trixie was stuck. What she knew about computers could have been written on the back of a postage stamp.

I should say something about this aunt of mine. She is large, with red hair 'out of a bottle' …that's what she says, and I suppose that means she dyes it, because I don't know about you, but I've never seen actual *hair* sold in bottles. She wears very loud colours.

"I like people to notice me," she says, and it would be impossible not to see her coming a mile off, with her yellow coat and her favourite purple tights. She used to live in a little flat above the launderette, but everything's changed now… you'll see why when I tell you about Stella and her magic.

As soon as they moved the machines into the library, Aunt Trixie enrolled in a 'Make friends with your Computer' class at the local college. It didn't take her long to get the hang of them, and the story that her teacher left with a nervous breakdown after three weeks of teaching Aunt Trixie is nothing but a rumour, put about by what she calls the Forces of Beigeness.

"You've heard about the Forces of Darkness, haven't you?" she said to me. "Well, these are far worse. They want to make the world safe and bland and beige… they can't stand colour and noise so they try to destroy anyone who isn't as beige as they are."

Have I mentioned that my Aunt Trixie is a little eccentric? I'm sure you'll have worked that out by now.

Anyway, Wednesday was her day for the library. She could be seen there every week, early in the afternoon, surfing away like mad. And Stella soon worked out that it was worthwhile leaving her armchair in the reference library, because Aunt Trixie always had a tidbit hidden somewhere about her person. As well as being eccentric and colourful and a brilliant Internet surfer, Aunt Trixie was a cat-lover.

One day, while Stella was sitting on the mouse mat (which Aunt Trixie called a Cat mat) next to her machine, a friend of Aunt Trixie's came into the library to see what was new and interesting. With cries of joy, the two friends started talking, and neither of them noticed Stella poking out a paw and pressing the keys from time to time. By the time Aunt Trixie's friend had gone, Stella was licking her paws contentedly, but on the screen, bright and clear, with no other words anywhere around it were the letters:

ME S CAT

Aunt Trixie blinked. "Did you type this, Stella?" she asked.

Stella looked at her out of pale green eyes, but said nothing. Aunt Trixie looked around. She had not typed the letters. The library was unusually quiet. Only Miss Thomson was there, bent over her own computer, behind the desk, checking to see which books had been taken out.

"You did, didn't you?" said Aunt Trixie. She blinked again and pressed a few buttons. "I'm going to print this out. It's evidence."

By the time the sheet slid into her hand, she realised that no one would believe she hadn't typed the letters in herself.

"But we know, don't we, Stella? We won't tell anyone. I'll just keep this safe."

Now there's one thing about Aunt Trixie I haven't told you yet. She's a mad Lottery fan. She does it every Wednesday – only one game, mind you, because she's not daft. She left the library with Stella's message in her bag, and went straight to the newsagent's to buy her ticket. How, she wondered, could she make use of the magical message she felt sure Stella had sent her?

"I've got it!" she said to the newsagent when she got there. "I'll change the letters into numbers!"

The newsagent smiled. He had no idea what she meant. Once the letters were converted into numbers they looked like this: 13, 5, 19, 3, 1, 20… or in Lottery order: 1, 3, 5, 13, 19, 20.

It was a rollover that night. Aunt Trixie was the only person in the country who chose a set of numbers based on what a cat with magic powers had typed on her computer screen while she was busy gossiping. Aunt Trixie won £4,000,000 and now lives in a pink and white meringue of a house in Miami, where the Forces of Beigeness are unknown. She gave my mum lots of money, too, so we've moved to a bigger house, but we'd never go anywhere too far away from the library where Stella still lives. As far as we know, no one else has benefited from her magic, but I have a go on the computers every now and then, just in case. Stella sometimes comes and sits on my Cat mat, but she seems to have given up typing, for the moment...

The Wind in the Willows

by Kenneth Grahame

When Mole abandons his spring-cleaning, and sets out across the meadows, his wanderings lead him to the river and a whole new set of friends. He takes an instant liking to Ratty, with whom he agrees to spend the summer, learning about boating, swimming and the endless fads of the flamboyant Mr Toad.

"Ratty," said the Mole suddenly, one bright summer morning, "if you please, I want to ask you a favour."

The Rat was sitting on the river bank, singing a little song. He had just composed it himself, so he was very taken up with it, and would not pay proper attention to Mole or anything else. Since early morning he had been swimming in the river, in company with his friends the ducks. And when the ducks stood on their heads suddenly, as ducks will, he would dive down and tickle their necks, just under where their chins would be if ducks had chins, till they were forced to come to the surface again in a hurry, spluttering and angry and shaking their feathers at him, for it is impossible to say quite *all* you feel when your head is under water. At last they implored him to go away and attend to his own affairs and leave them to mind theirs. So the Rat went away, and sat on the river bank in the sun, and made up a song about them, which he called:

Ducks' Ditty

All along the backwater,
Through the rushes tall,
Ducks are a-dabbling,
Up tails all!

Ducks' tails, drakes' tails,
Yellow feet a-quiver,
Yellow bills all out of sight
Busy in the river!

Slushy green undergrowth
Where the roach swim –
Here we keep our larder,
Cool and full and dim.

Every one for what he likes!
We like to be
Heads down, tails up,
Dabbling free!

High in the blue above
Swifts whirl and call –
We are down a-dabbling,
Up tails all!

"I don't know that I think so *very* much of that little song, Rat," observed the Mole cautiously. He was no poet himself and didn't care who knew it; and he had a candid nature.

"Nor don't the ducks neither," replied the Rat cheerfully. "They say, '*Why* can't fellows be allowed to do what they like *when* they like and *as* they like, instead of other fellows sitting on banks and watching them all the time and making remarks and poetry and things about them? What *nonsense* it all is!' That's what the ducks say."

"So it is, so it is," said the Mole, with great heartiness.

"No, it isn't!" cried the Rat indignantly.

"Well then, it isn't, it isn't," replied the Mole soothingly. "But what I wanted to ask you was, won't you take me to call on Mr Toad? I've heard so much about him, and I do so want to make his acquaintance."

"Why, certainly," said the good-natured Rat, jumping to his feet and dismissing poetry from his mind for the day. "Get the boat out, and we'll paddle up there at once. It's never the wrong time to call on Toad. Early or late he's always the same fellow. Always good-tempered, always glad to see you, always sorry when you go!"

"He must be a very nice animal," observed the Mole, as he got into the boat and took the sculls, while the Rat settled himself comfortably in the stern.

"He is indeed the best of animals," replied Rat. "So simple, so good-natured, and so affectionate. Perhaps he's not very clever – we can't all be geniuses; and it may be that he is both boastful and conceited. But he has got some great qualities, has Toady."

Rounding a bend in the river, they came in sight of a handsome, dignified old house of mellowed red brick, with well-kept lawns reaching down to the water's edge.

"There's Toad Hall," said the Rat; "and that creek on the left, where the notice-board says 'Private. No landing allowed', leads to his boat-house, where we'll leave the boat. The stables are over there to the right. That's the banqueting-hall you're looking at now – very old, that is. Toad is rather rich, you know, and this is really one of the nicest houses in these parts, though we never admit as much to Toad."

They glided up the creek, and the Mole shipped his sculls as they passed into the shadow of a large boat-house. Here they saw many handsome boats, slung from the cross-beams or hauled up on a slip, but none in the water; and the place had an unused and a deserted air.

The Rat looked around him. "I understand," said he. "Boating is played out. He's tired of it, and done with it. I wonder what new fad he has taken up now? Come along and let's look him up. We shall hear all about it quite soon enough."

They disembarked, and strolled across the gay flower-decked lawns in search of Toad, whom they presently happened upon resting in a wicker garden-chair, with a preoccupied expression of face, and a large map spread out on his knees.

"Hooray!" he cried, jumping up on seeing them, "this is splendid!" He shook the paws of both of them warmly, never waiting for an introduction to the Mole. "How *kind* of you!" he went on, dancing round them.

"I was just going to send a boat down the river for you, Ratty, with strict orders that you were to be fetched up here at once, whatever you were doing. I want you badly – both of you. Now what will you take? Come inside and have something! You don't know how lucky it is, your turning up just now!"

"Let's sit quiet a bit, Toady!" said the Rat, throwing himself into an easy chair, while the Mole took another by the side of him and made some civil remark about Toad's 'delightful residence'.

"Finest house on the whole river," cried Toad boisterously. "Or anywhere else, for that matter," he could not help adding.

Here the Rat nudged the Mole. Unfortunately the Toad saw him do it, and turned very red. There was a moment's painful silence. Then Toad burst out laughing. "All right, Ratty," he said. "It's only my way, you know. And it's not such a very bad house, is it? You know you rather like it yourself. Now, look here. Let's be sensible. You are the very animals I wanted. You've got to help me. It's most important!"

"It's about your rowing, I suppose," said the Rat, with an innocent air. "You're getting on fairly well, though you splash a good bit still. With a great deal of patience, and any quantity of coaching, you may –"

"O, pooh! boating!" interrupted the Toad, in great disgust. "Silly boyish amusement. I've given that up *long* ago. Sheer waste of time, that's what it is. It makes me downright sorry to see you fellows, who ought to know better, spending all your energies in that aimless manner. No, I've discovered the real thing, the only genuine occupation for a lifetime. I propose to devote the remainder of mine to it, and can only regret the wasted years that lie behind me, squandered in trivialities. Come with me, dear Ratty, and your amiable friend also, if he will be so very good, just as far as the stable-yard, and you shall see what you shall see!"

He led the way to the stable-yard accordingly, the Rat following with a most mistrustful expression; and there, drawn out of the coach-house into the open, they saw a gipsy caravan, shining with newness, painted a canary-yellow picked out with green, and red wheels.

"There you are!" cried the Toad, straddling and expanding himself. "There's real life for you, embodied in that little cart. The open road, the dusty highway, the heath, the common, the hedgerows, the rolling downs! Camps, villages, towns, cities! Here today, up and off to somewhere else tomorrow! Travel, change, interest, excitement! The whole world before you, and a horizon that's always changing! And mind, this is the very finest cart of its sort that was ever built, without any exception. Come inside and look at the arrangements. Planned 'em all myself, I did!"

The Mole was tremendously interested and excited, and followed him eagerly up the steps and into the interior of the caravan. The Rat only snorted and thrust his hands deep into his pockets, remaining where he was.

It was indeed very compact and comfortable. Little sleeping-bunks – a little table that folded up against the wall – a cooking-stove, lockers, bookshelves, a bird-cage with a bird in it; and pots, pans, jugs and kettles of every size and variety.

"All complete!" said the Toad triumphantly, pulling open a locker. "You see – biscuits, potted lobster, sardines – everything you can possibly want. Soda-water here – baccy there – letter-paper, bacon, jam, cards and dominoes – you'll find," he continued, as they descended the steps again, "you'll find that nothing whatever has been forgotten, when we make our start this afternoon."

"I beg your pardon," said the Rat slowly, as he chewed a straw, "but did I overhear you say something about '*we*', and '*start*', and '*this afternoon*'?"

"Now, you dear good old Ratty," said Toad imploringly, "don't begin talking in that stiff and sniffy sort of way, because you know you've *got* to come. I can't possibly manage without you, so please consider it settled, and don't argue – it's the one thing I can't stand. You surely don't mean to stick to your dull fusty old river all your life, and just live in a hole in a bank, and *boat*? I want to show you the world! I'm going to make an *animal* of you, my boy!"

"I don't care," said the Rat doggedly. "I'm not coming, and that's flat. And I am going to stick to my old river, *and* live in a hole, *and* boat, as I've always done. And what's more, Mole's going to stick to me and do as I do, aren't you, Mole?"

"Of course I am," said the Mole loyally. "I'll always stick to you, Rat, and what you say is to be – has got to be. All the same, it sounds as if it might have been – well, rather fun, you know!" he added wistfully. Poor Mole! The Life Adventurous was so new a thing to him and so thrilling; and this fresh aspect of it was so tempting; and he had fallen in love at first sight with the canary-coloured cart and all its little fitments.

The Rat saw what was passing in his mind, and wavered. He hated disappointing people, and he was fond of the Mole, and would do almost anything to oblige him. Toad was watching both of them closely.

"Come along in and have some lunch," he said diplomatically, "and we'll talk it over. We needn't decide anything in a hurry. Of course, I don't really care. I only want to give pleasure to you fellows. 'Live for others!' That's my motto in life."

During luncheon – which was excellent, of course, as everything at Toad Hall always was – the Toad simply let himself go. Disregarding the Rat, he proceeded to play upon the inexperienced Mole as on a harp. Naturally a voluble animal, and always mastered by his imagination, he painted the prospects of the trip and the joys of the open life and the roadside in such glowing colours that the Mole could hardly sit in his chair for excitement. Somehow, it soon seemed taken for granted by all three of them that the trip was a settled thing; and the Rat, though still unconvinced in his mind, allowed his good-nature to over-ride his personal objections. He could not bear to disappoint his two friends, who were already deep in schemes and anticipations, planning out each day's separate occupation for several weeks ahead.

When they were quite ready, the now triumphant Toad led his companions to the paddock and set them to capture the old grey horse, who, without having been consulted, and to his own extreme annoyance, had been told off by Toad for the dustiest job in this dusty expedition. He frankly preferred the paddock, and took a deal of catching. Meantime Toad packed the lockers still tighter with necessaries, and hung nose-bags, nets of onions, bundles of hay, and baskets from the bottom of the cart. At last the horse was caught and harnessed, and they set off, all talking at once, each animal either trudging by the side of the cart or sitting on the shaft, as the humour took him. It was a golden afternoon. The smell of the dust they kicked up was rich and satisfying; out of thick orchards on either side the road, birds called and whistled to them cheerily; good-natured wayfarers, passing them, gave them "Good day", or stopped to say nice things about their beautiful cart; and rabbits, sitting at their front doors in the hedgerows, held up their forepaws, and said, "O my! O my! O my!"

Late in the evening, tired and happy and miles from home, they drew up on a remote common far from habitations, turned the horse loose to graze, and ate their simple supper sitting on the grass by the side of the cart. Toad talked big about all he was going to do in the days to come, while stars grew fuller and larger all around them, and a yellow moon, appearing suddenly and silently from nowhere in particular, came to keep them company and listen to their talk. At last they turned into their little bunks in the cart; and Toad, kicking out his legs, sleepily said, "Well, good night, you fellows! This is the real life for a gentleman! Talk about your old river!"

"I *don't* talk about my river," replied the patient Rat. "You *know* I don't, Toad. But I *think* about it," he added pathetically, in a lower tone: "I think about it – all the time!"

The Mole reached out from under his blanket, felt for the Rat's paw in the darkness, and gave it a squeeze. "I'll do whatever you like, Ratty," he whispered. "Shall we run away tomorrow morning, quite early – *very* early – and go back to our dear old hole on the river?"

"No, no, we'll see it out," whispered back the Rat. "Thanks awfully, but I ought to stick by Toad till this trip is ended. It wouldn't be safe for him to be left to himself. It won't take very long. His fads never do. Good night!"

The end was indeed nearer than even the Rat suspected.

After so much open air and excitement the Toad slept very soundly, and no amount of shaking could rouse him out of bed next morning. So the Mole and Rat turned to, quietly and manfully, and while the Rat saw to the horse, and lit a fire, and cleaned last night's cups and platters, and got things ready for breakfast, the Mole trudged off to the nearest village, a long way off, for milk and eggs and various necessaries the Toad had, of course, forgotten to provide. The hard work had all been done, and the two animals were resting, thoroughly exhausted, by the time Toad appeared on the scene, fresh and gay, remarking what a pleasant easy life it was they were all leading now, after the cares and worries and fatigues of housekeeping at home.

They had a pleasant ramble that day over grassy downs and along narrow by-lanes, and camped, as before, on a common, only this time the two guests took care that Toad should do his fair share of work. In consequence, when the time came for starting next morning, Toad was by no means so rapturous about the simplicity of the primitive life, and indeed attempted to resume his place in his bunk, whence he was hauled by force. Their way lay, as before, across country by narrow lanes, and it was not till the afternoon that they came out on the high road, their first high road; and there disaster, fleet and unforeseen, sprang out on them – disaster momentous indeed to their expedition, but simply overwhelming in its effect on the after-career of Toad.

They were strolling along the high road easily, the Mole by the horse's head, talking to him, since the horse had complained that he was being frightfully left out of it, and nobody considered him in the least; the Toad and the Water Rat walking behind the cart talking together – at least Toad was talking, and Rat was saying at intervals, "Yes, precisely; and what did *you* say to *him*?" – and thinking all the time of something very different, when far behind them they heard a faint warning hum, like the drone of a distant bee. Glancing back, they saw a small cloud of dust, with a dark centre of energy, advancing on them at incredible speed, while from out of the dust a faint 'Poop-poop!' wailed like an uneasy animal in pain. Hardly regarding it, they turned to resume their conversation, when in an instant (as it seemed) the peaceful scene was changed, and with a blast of wind and a whirl of sound that made them jump for the nearest ditch, it was on them! The 'poop-poop' rang with a brazen shout in their ears, they had a moment's glimpse of an interior of glittering plate-glass and rich morocco, and the magnificent motor-car, immense, breath-snatching, passionate, with its pilot tense and hugging his wheel, possessed all earth and air for the fraction of a second, flung an enveloping cloud of dust that blinded and enwrapped them utterly, and then dwindled to a speck in the far distance, changed back into a droning bee once more.

The old grey horse, dreaming, as he plodded along, of his quiet paddock, in a new raw situation such as this simply abandoned himself to his natural emotions. Rearing, plunging, backing steadily, in spite of all the Mole's efforts at his head, and all the Mole's lively language directed at his better feelings, he drove the cart backwards towards the deep ditch at the side of the road. It wavered an instant – then there was a heartrending crash – and the canary-coloured cart, their pride and their joy, lay on its side in the ditch, an irredeemable wreck.

The Rat danced up and down in the road, simply transported with passion. "You villains!" he shouted, shaking both fists. "You scoundrels, you highwaymen you – you – road-hogs! – I'll have the law on you! I'll report you! I'll take you through all the Courts!"

His home-sickness had quite slipped away from him, and for the moment he was the skipper of the canary-coloured vessel driven on a shoal by the reckless jockeying of rival mariners, and he was trying to recollect all the fine and biting things he used to say to masters of steam-launches when their wash, as they drove too near the bank, used to flood his parlour carpet at home.

Toad sat straight down in the middle of the dusty road, his legs stretched out before him, and stared fixedly in the direction of the disappearing motor-car. He breathed short, his face wore a placid, satisfied expression, and at intervals he faintly murmured, "Poop-poop!"

The Mole was busy trying to quiet the horse, which he succeeded in doing after a time. Then he went to look at the cart, on its side in the ditch. It was indeed a sorry sight. Panels and windows smashed, axles hopelessly bent, one wheel off, sardine-tins scattered over the wide world, and the bird in the bird-cage sobbing pitifully and calling to be let out.

The Rat came to help him, but their united efforts were not sufficient to right the cart. "Hi! Toad!" they cried. "Come and bear a hand, can't you!"

The Toad never answered a word, or budged from his seat in the road; so they went to see what was the matter with him. They found him in a sort of trance, a happy smile on his face, his eyes still fixed on the dusty wake of their destroyer. At intervals he was still heard to murmur "Poop-poop!"

The Rat shook him by the shoulder. "Are you coming to help us, Toad?" he demanded sternly.

"Glorious, stirring sight!" murmured Toad, never offering to move. "The poetry of motion! The *real* way to travel! The *only* way to travel! Here today – in next week tomorrow! Villages skipped, towns and cities jumped – always somebody else's horizon! O bliss! O poop-poop! O my! O my!"

"O, *stop* being an ass, Toad!" cried the Mole despairingly.

"And to think I never *knew*!" went on the Toad in a dreamy monotone. "All those wasted years that lie behind me, I never knew, never even *dreamt*! But *now* – but now that I know, now that I fully realise! O what a flowery track lies spread before me, henceforth! What dust-clouds shall spring up behind me as I speed on my reckless way! What carts I shall fling carelessly into the ditch in the wake of my magnificent onset! Horrid little carts – common carts – canary-coloured carts!"

"What are we to do with him?" asked the Mole of the Water Rat.

"Nothing at all," replied the Rat firmly. "Because there is really nothing to be done. You see, I know him from of old. He is now possessed. He has got a new craze, and it always takes him that way, in its first stage. He'll continue like that for days now, like an animal walking in a happy dream, quite useless for all practical purposes. Never mind him. Let's go and see what there is to be done about the cart."

A careful inspection showed them that, even if they succeeded in righting it by themselves, the cart would travel no longer. The axles were in a hopeless state, and the missing wheel was shattered into pieces.

The Rat knotted the horse's reins over his back and

took him by the head, carrying the bird-cage and its hysterical occupant in the other hand. "Come on!" he said grimly to the Mole. "It's five or six miles to the nearest town, and we shall just have to walk it. The sooner we make a start the better."

"But what about Toad?" asked the Mole anxiously, as they set off together. "We can't leave him here, sitting in the middle of the road by himself, in the distracted state he's in! It's not safe. Supposing another Thing were to come along?"

"O, *bother* Toad," said the Rat savagely; "I've done with him!"

They had not proceeded very far on their way, however, when there was a pattering of feet behind them, and Toad caught them up and thrust a paw inside the elbow of each of them; still breathing short and staring into vacancy.

"Now, look here, Toad!" said the Rat sharply: "as soon as we get to the town, you'll have to go straight to the police-station, and see if they know anything about that motor-car and who it belongs to, and lodge a complaint against it. And then you'll have to go to a blacksmith's or a wheelwright's and arrange for the cart to be fetched and mended and put to rights. It'll take time, but it's not quite a hopeless smash. Meanwhile, the Mole and I will go to an inn and find comfortable rooms where we can stay till the cart's ready, and till your nerves have recovered from their shock."

"Police-station! Complaint!" murmured Toad dreamily. "Me *complain* of that beautiful, that heavenly vision that has been vouchsafed me! *Mend* the *cart*! I've done with carts for ever. I never want to see the cart, or to hear of it again. O, Ratty! You can't think how obliged I am to you for consenting to come on this trip! I wouldn't have gone without you, and then I might never have seen that – that swan, that sunbeam, that thunderbolt! I might never have heard that entrancing sound, or smelt that bewitching smell! I owe it all to you, my best of friends!"

The Rat turned from him in despair. "You see what it is?" he said to the Mole, addressing him across Toad's head: "He's quite hopeless. I give it up – when we get to the town we'll go to the railway-station, and with luck we may pick up a train there that'll get us back to River Bank tonight. And if ever you catch me going a-pleasuring with this provoking animal again!" – He snorted, and during the rest of that weary trudge addressed his remarks exclusively to Mole.

On reaching the town they went straight to the station and deposited Toad in the second-class waiting-room, giving a porter twopence to keep a strict eye on him. They then left the horse at an inn stable, and gave what directions they could about the cart and its contents. Eventually, a slow train having landed them at a station not very far from Toad Hall, they escorted the spellbound, sleep-walking Toad to his door, put him inside it, and instructed his housekeeper to feed him, undress him, and put him to bed. Then they got out their boat from the boat-house, sculled down the river home, and at a very late hour sat down to supper in their own cosy riverside parlour, to the Rat's great joy and contentment.

The following evening the Mole, who had risen late and taken things very easy all day, was sitting on the bank fishing, when the Rat, who had been looking up his friends and gossiping, came strolling along to find him. "Heard the news?" he said. "There's nothing else being talked about, all along the river bank. Toad went up to Town by an early train this morning. And he has ordered a large and very expensive motor-car."

The Magic Pudding

by Norman Lindsay

Bunyip Bluegum sets off to see the world to escape from his Uncle Wattleberry, and not long after he meets Bill Barnacle the sailor and Sam Sawnoff the penguin who are tucking into a nice big steak-and-kidney pudding. What he is not prepared for is that this is a magic pudding, which grows back after every mouthful, and therefore is much sought after...

The Society of Puddin'-Owners were up bright and early next morning, and had the billy on and tea made before six o'clock, which is the best part of the day, because the world has just had his face washed, and the air smells like Pears' soap.

"Aha," said Bill Barnacle, cutting up slices of the Puddin', "this is what I call grand. Here we are, after a splendid night's sleep on dry leaves, havin' a smokin' hot slice of steak-and-kidney for breakfast round the camp fire. What could be more delightful?"

"What indeed?" said Bunyip Bluegum, sipping his tea.

"Why, as I always say," said Bill, "if there's one thing

more entrancin' than sittin' round a camp fire in the evenin' it's sittin' round a camp fire in the mornin'. No beds and blankets and breakfast tables for Bill Barnacle. For as I says in my 'Breakfast Ballad'—

"If there's anythin' better than lyin' on leaves,
It's risin' from leaves at dawnin',
If there's anythin' better than sleepin' at eve,
It's wakin' up in the mawnin'.

"If there's anythin' better than camp firelight,
It's bright sunshine on wakin'.
If there's anythin' better than puddin' at night,
It's puddin' when day is breakin'.

"If there's anythin' better than singin' away
While the stars are gaily shinin',
Why, it's singin' a song at dawn of day,
On puddin' for breakfast dinin'."

There was a hearty round of applause at this song, for, as Bunyip Bluegum remarked, "Singing at breakfast should certainly be more commonly indulged in, as it greatly tends to enliven what is on most occasions a somewhat dull proceeding."

"One of the great advantages of being a professional puddin'-owner," said Sam Sawnoff, "is that songs at breakfast are always encouraged. None of the ordinary breakfast rules such as scowling while eating, and saying the porridge is as stiff as glue and the eggs are as tough as leather, are observed. Instead, songs, roars of laughter, and boisterous jests are the order of the day. For example, this sort of thing," added Sam, doing a rapid back-flip and landing with a thump on Bill's head. As Bill was unprepared for this act of boisterous humour, his face was pushed into the Puddin' with great violence, and the gravy was splashed in his eye.

"What d'yer mean, playin' such bungfoodlin' tricks on a man at breakfast?" roared Bill.

"What d'yer mean," shouted the Puddin', "playing such foodbungling tricks on a Puddin' being breakfasted at?"

"Breakfast humour, Bill, merely breakfast humour," said Sam hastily.

"Humour's humour," shouted Bill, "but puddin' in the whiskers is no joke."

"Whiskers in the Puddin' is worse than puddin' in the whiskers," shouted the Puddin', standing up in his basin.

"Observe the rules, Bill," said Sam hurriedly. "Boisterous humour at the breakfast table must be greeted with roars of laughter."

"To Jeredelum with the rules," shouted Bill. "Pushing a man's face into his own breakfast is beyond rules or reason, and deserves a punch in the gizzard."

Seeing matters arriving at this unpromising situation, Bunyip Bluegum interposed by saying, "Rather than allow this happy occasion to be marred by unseemly recriminations, let us, while admitting that our admirable friend, Sam, may have unwittingly disturbed the composure of our admirable friend, Bill, at the expense of our admirable Puddin's gravy, let us, I say, by the simple act of extending the hand of friendship, dispel in an instant these gathering clouds of disruption. In the words of the poem—

> "Then let the fist of Friendship
> Be kept for Friendship's foes.
> Ne'er let that hand in anger land
> On Friendship's holy nose."

These fine sentiments at once dispelled Bill's anger. He shook hands warmly with Sam, wiped the gravy from his face, and resumed breakfast with every appearance of hearty good humour.

The meal over, the breakfast things were put away in the bag, Sam and Bill took Puddin' between them, and all set off along the road, enlivening the way with song and story. Bill regaled them with portions of the 'Ballad of the *Salt Junk Sarah*', which is one of those songs that go on for ever. Its great advantage, as Bill remarked, was that as it hadn't got an ending it didn't need a beginning, so you could start it anywhere.

"As for instance," said Bill, and he roared out—

> "Ho, aboard the *Salt Junk Sarah*,
> Rollin' home across the line,
> The Bo'sun collared the Captain's hat
> And threw it in the brine.
> Rollin' home, rollin' home,
> Rollin' home across the foam,
> The Captain sat without a hat
> The whole way rollin' home."

Entertaining themselves in this way as they strolled

along, they were presently arrested by shouts of "Fire! Fire!" and a Fireman in a large helmet came bolting down the road, pulling a fire hose behind him.

"Aha!" said Bill. "Now we shall have the awe-inspirin' spectacle of a fire to entertain us," and, accosting the Fireman, he demanded to know where the fire was.

"The fact is," said the Fireman, "that owing to the size of this helmet I can't see where it is; but if you will kindly glance at the surrounding district, you'll see it about somewhere."

They glanced about and, sure enough, there was a fire burning in the next field. It was only a cowshed, certainly, but it was blazing very nicely, and well worth looking at.

"Fire," said Bill, "in the form of a common cowshed, is burnin' about nor'-nor'-east as the crow flies."

"In that case," said the Fireman, "I invite all present to bravely assist in putting it out. But," he added impressively, "if you'll take my advice, you'll shove that Puddin' in this hollow log and roll a stone agen the end to keep him in, for if he gets too near the flames he'll be cooked again and have his flavour ruined."

"This is a very sensible feller," said Bill, and though Puddin' objected strongly, he was at once pushed into a log and securely fastened in with a large stone.

"How'd you like to be shoved in a blooming log," he shouted at Bill, "when you was burning with anxiety to see the fire?" but Bill said severely, "Be sensible, Albert, fires is too dangerous to Puddin's flavours."

No more time was lost in seizing the hose and they

set off with the greatest enthusiasm. For, as everyone knows, running with the reel is one of the grand joys of being a fireman. They had the hose fixed to a garden tap in no time, and soon were all hard at work, putting out the fire.

Of course there was a great deal of smoke and shouting, and getting tripped up by the hose, and it was by the merest chance Bunyip Bluegum glanced back in time to see the Wombat in the act of stealing the Puddin' from the hollow log.

"Treachery is at work," he shouted.

"Treachery," roared Bill, and with one blow on the snout knocked the Fireman endways on into the burning cinders, where his helmet fell off, and exposed the countenance of that snooting, snouting scoundrel, the Possum.

The Possum, of course, hadn't expected to have his disguise pierced so swiftly, and, though he managed to scramble out of the fire in time to save his bacon, he was considerably singed down the back.

"What a murderous attack!" he exclaimed. "O, what a brutal attempt to burn a man alive!" And as some hot cinders had got down his back he gave a sharp yell and ran off, singeing and smoking. Bill, distracted with rage, ran after the Possum, then changed his mind and ran after the Wombat, so that, what with running first after one and then after the other, they both had time to get clean away, and disappeared over the skyline.

"I see it all," shouted Bill, casting himself down in despair. "Them low puddin'-thieves has borrowed a fireman's helmet, collared a hose, an' set fire to a cowshed in order to lure us away from the Puddin'."

"The whole thing's a low put-up job on our noble credulity," said Sam, casting himself down beside Bill.

"It's one of the most frightful things that's ever happened," said Bill.

"It's worse than treading on tacks with bare feet," said Sam.

"It's worse than bein' caught stealin' fowls," said Bill.

"It's worse than bein' stood on by cows," said Sam.

"It's almost as bad as havin' an uncle called Aldobrantifoscofornio," said Bill, and they both sang loudly—

"It's worse than weevils, worse than warts,
It's worse than corns to bear.
It's worse than havin' several quarts
Of treacle in your hair.

"It's worse than beetles in the soup,
It's worse than crows to eat.
It's worse than wearin' small-sized boots
Upon your large-sized feet.

"It's worse than kerosene to boose,
It's worse than ginger hair.
It's worse than anythin' to lose
A Puddin' rich and rare."

Bunyip Bluegum reproved this despondency, saying, "Come, come, this is no time for giving way to despair. Let us, rather, by the fortitude of our bearing prove ourselves superior to this misfortune and, with the energy of justly enraged men, pursue these malefactors, who have so richly deserved our vengeance. Arise!

"The grass is green, the day is fair,
The dandelions abound.
Is this a time for sad despair
And sitting on the ground?

"Let gloom give way to angry glare,
Let weak despair be drowned,
Let vengeance in its rage declare
Our Puddin' must be found.

"Our Puddin' in some darksome lair
In iron chains is bound,
While puddin'-snatchers on him fare,
And eat him by the pound.

"Then let's resolve to do and dare.
Let teeth with rage be ground.
Let voices to the heavens declare
Our Puddin' MUST be found."

"Bravely spoken," said Bill, immediately recovering from despair.

"Those gallant words have fired our blood," said Sam, and they both shook hands with Bunyip, to show that they were now prepared to follow the call of vengeance.

"In order to investigate this dastardly outrage," said Bunyip, "we must become detectives, and find a clue. We must find somebody who has seen a singed possum. Once traced to their lair, mother-wit will suggest some means of rescuing our Puddin'.'"

They set off at once, and, after a brisk walk, came to a small house with a signboard on it saying 'Henderson Hedgehog, Horticulturist'. Henderson himself was in the garden, horticulturing a cabbage, and they asked him if he had chanced to see a singed possum that morning.

"What's that? What, what?" said Henderson Hedgehog, and when they had repeated the question, he said, "You must speak up, I'm a trifle deaf."

"Have you seen a singed possum?" shouted Bill.

"I can't hear you," said Henderson.

"Have you seen a SINGED POSSUM?" roared Bill.

"To be sure," said Henderson, "but the turnips are backward."

"Turnips be stewed," yelled Bill in such a tremendous voice that he blew his own hat off. "HAVE YOU SEEN A SINGED POSSUM?"

"Good season for wattle blossom," said Henderson. "Well, yes, but a very poor season for carrots."

"A man might as well talk to a carrot as try an' get sense out of this runt of a feller," said Bill, disgusted. "Come an' see if we can't find someone that it won't bust a man's vocal cords gettin' information out of."

They left Henderson to his horticulturing and walked on till they met a Parrot who was a Swagman, or a Swagman who was a Parrot. He must have been one or the other, if not both, for he had a bag and a swag, and a beak and a billy, and a thundering bad temper into the bargain, for the moment Bill asked him if he had met a singed possum he shouted back:

"Me eat a singed possum! I wouldn't eat a possum if he was singed, roasted, boiled, or fried."

"Not ett – met," shouted Bill. "I said, met a singed possum."

"Why can't yer speak plainly, then," said the Parrot. "Have you got a fill of tabacco on yer?"

He took out his pipe and scowled at Bill.

"Here you are," said Bill. "Cut a fill an' answer the question."

"All in good time," said the Parrot, and he added to Sam, "You got any tobacco?"

Sam handed him a fill, and he put it in his pocket. "You ain't got any tobacco," he said scornfully to Bunyip Bluegum. "I can see that at a glance. You're one of the non-smoking sort, all fur and feathers."

"Here," said Bill angrily, "enough o' this beatin' about the bush. Answer the question."

"Don't be impatient," said the Parrot. "Have you got a bit o' tea an' sugar on yer?"

"Here's yer tea an' sugar," said Bill, handing a little of each out of the bag. "An' that's the last thing you get. Now will you answer the question?"

"Wot question?" asked the Parrot.

"Have yer seen a singed possum?" roared Bill.

"No, I haven't," said the Parrot, and he actually had the insolence to laugh in Bill's face.

"Of all the swivel-eyed, up-jumped, cross-grained, sons of a cock-eyed tinker," exclaimed Bill, boiling with rage. "If punching parrots on the beak wasn't too painful for pleasure, I'd land you a sockdolager on the muzzle that ud lay you out till Christmas. Come on, mates," he added, "it's no use wastin' time over this low-down, hook-nosed, tobacco-grabber." And leaving the evil-minded Parrot to pursue his evil-minded way, they hurried off in search of information.

The next person they spied was a Bandicoot carrying a watermelon. At a first glance you would have thought it was merely a watermelon walking by itself, but a second glance would have shown you that the walking was being done by a small pair of legs attached to the watermelon, and a third glance would have disclosed that the legs were attached to a Bandicoot.

They shouted, "Hi, you with the melon!" to attract his attention, and set off running after him, and the Bandicoot, being naturally of a terrified disposition, ran for all he was worth. He wasn't worth much as a runner, owing to the weight of the watermelon, and they caught him up half-way across the field.

Conceiving that his hour had come, the Bandicoot gave a shrill squeak of terror and fell on his knees.

"Take me watermelon," he gasped, "but spare me life."

"Stuff an' nonsense," said Bill. "We don't want your life. What we want is some information. Have you seen a singed possum about this morning?"

"Singed possums, sir, yes sir, certainly sir," gasped the Bandicoot, trembling violently.

"What," exclaimed Bill. "Do yer mean to say you have seen a singed possum?"

"Singed possums, sir, yes sir," gulped the Bandicoot. "Very plentiful, sir, this time of the year, sir, owing to the bush fires, sir."

"Rubbish," roared Bill. "I don't believe he's seen a singed possum at all."

"No, sir," quavered the Bandicoot. "Certainly not, sir. Wouldn't think of seeing singed possums if there was any objection, sir."

"You're a poltroon," shouted Bill. "You're a slaverin', quaverin', melon-carryin' nincompoop. There's no more chance of getting information out of you than out of a terrified Turnip."

Leaving the Bandicoot to pursue his quavering, melon-humping existence, they set off again, Bill giving way to some very despondent expressions.

"As far as I can see," he said, "if we can't find somethin' better than stone-deaf hedgehogs, peevish parrots and funkin' bandicoots we may as well give way to despair."

Bunyip Bluegum was forced to exert his finest oratory to inspire them to another frame of mind. "Let it never be said," he exclaimed, "that the unconquerable hearts of puddin'-owners quailed before a parrot, a hedgehog, or a bandicoot.

"Let hedgehogs deaf go delve and dig,
Immune from loudest howl,
Let bandicoots lump melons big,
Let peevish parrots prowl.

"Shall puddin'-owners bow the head
At such affronts as these?
No, no! March on, by anger led,
Our Puddin' to release.

"Let courage high resolve inflame
Our captive Pud to free;

66

Our banner wave, our words proclaim
We march to victory!"

"Bravely sung," exclaimed Bill, grasping Bunyip Bluegum by the hand, and they proceeded with expressions of the greatest courage and determination.

As a reward for this renewed activity, they got some useful information from a Rooster who was standing at his front gate looking up and down the road, and wishing to heaven that somebody would come along for him to talk to. They got, in fact, a good deal more information than they asked for, for the Rooster was one of those fine upstanding, bumptious skites who love to talk all day, in the heartiest manner, to total strangers while their wives do the washing.

"Singed possum," he exclaimed, when they had put the usual question to him. "Now, what an extraordinary thing that you should come along and ask me that question. What an astounding and incredible thing that you should actually use the word 'singed' in connection with the word 'possum'. Though mind you, the word I had in my mind was not 'singed', but 'burning'. And not 'possum' but 'feathers'. Now, I'll tell you why. Only this morning, as I was standing here, I said to myself, 'Somebody's been burning feathers'. I called out at once to the wife – fine woman, the wife, you'll meet her presently – 'Have you been burning feathers?' 'No,' says she. 'Well,' said I, 'if you haven't been burning feathers, somebody else has.' At the very moment that I'm repeating the word 'feathers' and 'burning' you come along and repeat the words 'singed' and 'possum'. Instantly I call to mind that at the identical moment that I smelt something burning, I saw a possum passing this very gate, though whether he happened to be singed or not I didn't inquire."

"Which way did he go?" inquired Bill excitedly.

"Now, let me see," said the Rooster. "He went down the road, turned to the right, gave a jump and a howl, and set off in the direction of Watkin Wombat's summer residence."

"The very man we're after," shouted Bill, and bolted off down the road, followed by the others, without taking any notice of the Rooster's request to wait a minute and be introduced to the wife.

"His wife may be all right," said Bill as they ran, "but what I say is, blow meetin' a bloomin' old Rooster's wife when you haven't got a year to waste listenin' to a bloomin' old Rooster."

They followed the Rooster's directions with the utmost rapidity, and came to a large hollow tree with a door in the side and a noticeboard nailed up which said 'Watkin Wombat, Esq., Summer Residence'.

The door was locked, but it was clear that the puddin'-thieves were inside, because they heard the Possum say peevishly, "You're eating too much, and here's me, most severely singed, not getting sufficient," and the Wombat was heard to say, "What you want is soap," but the Possum said angrily, "What I need is immense quantities of puddin'."

The avengers drew aside to hold a consultation.

"What's to be done?" said Bill. "It's no use knockin', because they'd look through the keyhole and refuse to come out, and, not bein' burglars, we can't bust the door in. It seems to me that there's nothin' for it but to give way to despair."

"Never give way to despair while whiskers can be made from dry grass," said Bunyip Bluegum, and suiting the action to the word, he swiftly made a pair of fine moustaches out of dried grass and stuck them on with wattle gum. "Now, lend me your hat," he said to Bill, and taking the hat he turned up the brim, dented in the top, and put it on. "The bag is also required," he said to Sam, and taking that in his hand and turning his coat inside out, he stood before them completely disguised.

"You two," he said, "must remain in hiding behind the tree. You will hear me knock, accost the ruffians and hold them in conversation. The moment you hear me exclaim loudly, 'Hey, Presto! Pots and Pans,' you will dart out and engage the villains at fisticuffs. The rest leave to me."

Waiting till the others were hidden behind the tree, Bunyip rapped smartly on the door which opened presently, and the Wombat put his head out cautiously.

"Have I the extreme pleasure of addressing Watkin Wombat, Esq.?" inquired Bunyip Bluegum, with a bow.

Of course, seeing a perfect stranger at the door, the Wombat had no suspicions, and said at once, "Such is the name of him you see before you."

"I have called to see you," said Bunyip, "on a matter of business. The commodity which I vend is Pootles' Patent Pudding Enlarger, samples of which I have in the bag. As a guarantee of good faith we are giving samples of our famous Enlarger away to all well-known puddin'-owners. The Enlarger, one of the wonders of modern science, has but to be poured over the puddin', with certain necessary incantations, and the puddin' will be instantly enlarged to double its normal size." He took some sugar from the bag and held it up. "I am now about to hand you some of this wonderful discovery. But," he added impressively, "the operation of enlarging the puddin' is a delicate one, and must be performed in the open air. Produce your puddin', and I will at once apply Pootles' Patent with marvellous effect."

"Of course it's understood that no charge is to be made," said the Possum, hurrying out.

"No charge whatever," said Bunyip Bluegum.

So on the principle of always getting something for nothing, as the Wombat said, Puddin' was brought out and placed on the ground.

"Now, watch me closely," said Bunyip Bluegum. He sprinkled the Puddin' with sugar, made several passes with his hands, and pronounced these words—

"Who incantations utters
He generally mutters
His gruesome blasts and bans.
But I, you need not doubt it,
Prefer aloud to shout it,
Hey, Presto! Pots and Pans."

Out sprang Bill and Sam and set about the puddin'-thieves like a pair of windmills, giving them such a clip clap clouting and a flip flap flouting, that what with being punched and pounded, and clipped and clapped, they had only enough breath left to give two shrieks of despair while scrambling back into Watkin Wombat's Summer Residence, and banging the door behind them. The three friends had Puddin' secured in no time, and shook hands all round, congratulating Bunyip Bluegum on the success of his plan.

"Your noble actin'," said Bill, "has saved our Puddin's life."

"Them puddin'-thieves," said Sam, "was children in your hands."

"We hear you," sang out the Possum, and the Wombat added, "Oh, what deceit!"

"Enough of you two," shouted Bill. "If we catch you sneakin' after our Puddin' again, you'll get such a beltin' that you'll wish you was vegetarians. And now," said he, "for a glorious reunion round the camp fire."

And a glorious reunion they had, tucking into hot steak-and-kidney puddin' and boiled jam roll, which, after the exertions of the day, went down, as Bill said, "Grand".

Seal Secret

by Aidan Chambers

*On holiday with his parents in Wales, William makes
friends with Gwyn. However he soon learns that his
new friend is in fact a tyrant and a bully, who has a
terrible secret: he is holding a seal pup captive in a cave
in order to start a seal farm. So William makes a brave
plan to rescue it…*

Next morning the sun rose at five twenty-three.
William saw it happen. By then he was already
approaching the cliff edge, where the meadow plunged
into the beach.

He was panting, and having to stop every few paces
to catch his breath and regain his strength. The bundle
he was carrying seemed five times heavier than when he
had tied it up in the junk shop yesterday afternoon.

Maybe, he thought, lying awake all night had left
him tired and weak. He had not dared let himself sleep
in case he did not wake in time. So all night long, he
had forced himself to stay awake, which had taken all
his concentration and willpower. Once or twice he had
dozed off, but luckily some part of his mind realised he

was drifting into unconsciousness each time and prodded him awake again.

At four-thirty he got up, dressed quickly, then stealthily climbed through his bedroom window into the cold dewy air of a misty, fretful morning. He shivered, as much from nervousness as from the chill.

But now, breathless and weak from dragging his bundle across two fields, he was sweating. The mist had soon cleared, leaving the sun shining from a cloudless sky. William was glad he would be on the beach in a few moments. Then his bundle could be blown up and the rest of the journey to the seal would be easy.

He struggled up the meadow bank to the cliff edge.

"Oh, heck!" he said aloud as soon as he saw the sea.

He had entirely forgotten the tide.

His plan supposed that the sea would be no higher up the beach than when Gwyn took him to the cave yesterday. But that had been later in the day, when the tide was almost as far out as it went. Now the sea covered the sand where he and Gwyn had played, and was furling among the pebbles. Which was bound to mean he could not wade across to the cave. The water would be too deep.

William looked anxiously around while his mind raced. How long would it be before the sea was far enough out to wade through? How long would it be before Gwyn came to check the seal? Would Gwyn get here before the sea was shallow enough? Everything depended on William reaching the cave and rescuing the seal before Gwyn arrived to stop him or to see where William took the pup.

William's idea was to wade to the cave pulling an inflatable dinghy behind him. He had found the little blow-up boat in the junk shop. It was the sort people played with in swimming pools, an imitation of the proper ones used by airmen when they crashed into the sea. William intended getting the seal somehow – he still wasn't quite sure how – into the dinghy which he would then tow along the shore well away from the cave, till he found a suitable place to hide the pup. Another cave maybe, but certainly somewhere unvisited that Gwyn wouldn't think of searching.

The pup could stay there until it wanted to go to sea. After all, William argued to himself, if the pup's mother had deserted what did it matter where the pup lived till its time came to swim away? So long as the place was not disturbed by people.

But he would have to do all this before Gwyn turned up. Last night the plan had seemed foolproof, neat and sound, and easier every time he thought of it. This morning, as he looked at the sea surging gently seventy feet below, his plan seemed anything but foolproof and far from easy. And difficult questions he had not thought of in the junk shop kept popping into his mind.

Suddenly he felt very lonely. He breathed in deeply to keep his stomach from heaving. Whatever he felt, he was still sure of one thing: no matter what happened, he was going to rescue that seal. There could be no turning back.

William took another deep breath. There was no point in hanging about on this cliff top. He was too visible. Someone might see him. His father going off to fish. Mr Davies perhaps. And that would be that: no rescue today or any day.

He picked up his bundle and went sliding and slithering down the cliff to the beach. He did not dare tumble the bundle down on its own because he was afraid a jagged stone might tear the dinghy's plastic skin. He wouldn't be able to blow it up at all then.

On the beach William stood for a moment surveying the sea. The water was flat calm. With the sun shining brightly from behind him, and with no breeze yet, everything was warm, peaceful, quiet. Except for the slur of slow waves scouring the pebbles. There weren't even any seagulls crying.

He began untying the bundle. Yesterday afternoon he had practised blowing the dinghy up. He had managed in just over a quarter of an hour of hard work, using a bicycle pump from one of the old bikes. Now, as he laid out the wrinkled skin, William decided that what he would do, as the tide was so high, was paddle the dinghy to the cave. He ought to be able to do that without trouble. And maybe by the time he got the seal aboard, the tide would be low enough for him to wade back, as he had planned, towing the dingy behind him.

He sat down, legs spread apart on either side of the dingy skin at the place where the nipple of the air valve was fixed. He attached the bicycle pump and began blowing.

Slowly – much slower, he was certain, than yesterday – the boat began taking shape, like a small bathtub with a fat tyre for walls.

When he had done at last, the dinghy firm and balloon bouncy, William glanced at his wrist watch. Ten minutes past six. His arms were aching from the effort. And he was feeling very hungry. He wished he had been able to eat breakfast before he set off, but that would have woken his parents.

He had to force himself on. Gwyn was sure to be up and about soon. Farmers started early in the day. He guessed that by seven o'clock Gwyn would be free to come to the cave, and it would take William all the time he had till then to do what had to be done.

He was glad to see that the water was a foot or two farther down the beach than it had been when he arrived. The sandy strip was beginning to show.

William tugged off his shoes and socks, stowed them in the dinghy's carrying bag with the pump, and hid the bag behind a big boulder at the base of the cliff.

He had brought a couple of hand paddles with him and a length of nylon rope. These he put into the dinghy, then pulled the boat carefully across the beach and into the sea. Its balloony weight rode on the surface as slippily as a bar of soap on ice.

This was the point of no return. William took in a deep breath, let it out in a long sigh, checked behind him that no one was watching, and thought, "Seal pup, here I come."

He almost threw himself into the boat, stomach down. The dinghy bobbed away seawards at an alarming speed. William hurriedly pushed his hands through the straps of the hand-paddles, and began scooping at the water.

At first the dinghy was hard to control. All William succeeded in doing was to turn in a crazy kind of circle that took him farther out to sea. Going in a straight line was the last thing the boat wanted to do. But after a few strokes, he found that with just the right strength in each he could keep the boat headed towards the cave.

Soon he was paddling with a steady rhythm. At each surge forward water slapped against the bow and sometimes sprayed into his face. It was like swimming the breaststroke without his body being in the water.

William began to enjoy the journey, pleased by his unexpected skill. He found himself wishing his father could see him doing so well. Maybe when the rescue was over, he would get his father to come to the beach and surprise him with a demonstration.

William's anxieties left him. He felt light-headed, confident; and the more confident he felt the quicker and more smoothly he managed to force the boat onward.

But as he rounded the bluff and entered the inlet, William noticed he was making slower progress, even though he was paddling as hard as ever. It was as though someone was pushing against the boat. To his left the island seemed to loom much bigger than it seemed from the shore.

He realised that the tide, funnelling out of the inlet and passing either side of the island, must be stronger here than along the open beach. If he stopped paddling he would be swept out to sea, or worse, wrecked on the rocky island.

Not a happy thought. William pushed it from his mind. Keeping his eyes fixed on his goal, he tried not to lose the steady rhythm of his strokes, even though the sea was rougher now. The boat wanted to slip and bob as each wave humped beneath it. He had to guess quickly what it would do next and how to keep it on course.

The hard work brought him out in a sweat. His mouth was dry and stiff-jawed. For a while he thought he was making no headway at all. Paddling became a dull, painful, mechanical movement. His arms ached. In his head he was pleading with himself to stop, just for a minute. But he knew if he did he would be dragged backwards by the tide. And any distance lost would be all the harder to make up again.

So he forced himself to keep going. And then when it seemed he really was getting nowhere, he saw that the cave was coming closer and closer, and that each stroke brought him nearer still.

At last, with a few extra-strong thrusts with the paddles, William managed to beach the dinghy in the cave mouth. He jumped ashore, pulled the boat out of the water, and slumped down on to the sand.

Never before had he felt such relief. Solid ground beneath him. An end to the grinding ache in his arms. The first stage of the rescue successfully finished. William smiled to himself.

When he had caught his breath, he sat up and looked across the water at the island and the long line of beach. The beach looked much farther away than it had seemed yesterday. He wondered how he had dared paddle across.

For a moment William felt twinges of guilt. Everyone – his father, his mother, Mr Davies, Miss James, even Gwyn – would say he had done something wrong. He knew that. He knew what he had done was dangerous. But he could not help revelling in his success.

Besides, William told himself, he had done it for the seal. He had no choice about it: he had to save the pup.

He got up, checked that the dinghy was safe from being washed away by any unusually high wave, and stepped quietly into the cave.

❧

This time William had no trouble seeing the pup. It was lying just where it had been yesterday. Gwyn must have worked on the wall after William left, for it was two or three layers of rock higher.

William looked at his watch. Six forty-five. No time to lose. This part of his plan he had thought out carefully, so he could work quickly. He began lifting rocks from the centre of the wall, throwing them away to his left. Soon he had made a gap wide enough to walk through.

His next job was to clear a path between the seal and the dinghy.

All along he had known that moving the seal would be the most difficult part of the rescue. William's first idea had been to carry the pup to the boat. But now, looking again at that roly-poly body, he knew he could not even lift it, never mind carry it twenty feet or more.

The pup was at least three feet long. But though it could twist a little and flap about with its flippers, he could see the pup was still too heavy for its own strength. And he knew it would not be able to turn and bite him, as long as he stayed behind its head.

William squatted on his haunches, his face as close to the pup's as he dared.

"It's all right," he said softly. "I'm not going to

hurt you."

The pup wriggled and snarled and began weeping.

"You might as well make up your mind," William went on, "I'm going to get you into that boat, and take you somewhere safe. Okay?"

The pup's eyes streamed tears. And the more it snapped and yowled and stretched its mouth, displaying its sharp teeth, the more the tears swamped its eyes.

"You're very beautiful, aren't you," William said, meaning it, "and I don't blame you for getting into a temper. But I've got to move you. For your own good."

He stood up, and scratched his head in thought.

"You're too heavy to pick up, see," he said. "And I daren't get near your front end. So I'm going to pull you down to the dinghy by your back flippers."

The pup snorted, as if clearing its nose.

"I wouldn't like it either," William said. "But I can't think of any other way." He paused, turning to look at the dinghy. "Trouble is," he said, "how do I get you in once we've reached the boat?"

During his long afternoon in the junk shop William had not been able to sort out this detail. He had hoped a solution would turn up when he was in the cave. But he still could not find one.

He sat on the wall, pondering the difficulty. With the dinghy lying on the ground, he would somehow have to lift the seal to get it over the boat's side.

Even if he could do that, he would then have to drag the boat, laden with the heavy pup, across the sand and into the sea. With the tide going out, that distance was growing longer every minute. What if the dinghy

80

wouldn't move at all? What if it snagged on a sharp rock?

William got up and went to the cave entrance. If only, he thought, there was a hole in the beach where the sea came, like a miniature dry dock. He could put the boat in and roll the seal off the sand into the boat.

But there was no such ready-made dock along the water's edge.

He stared out across the waves at the beach beyond, watching for any sign of movement. Frustration worried at his nerves. Well, he thought, gritting his teeth, if there wasn't a place to sink the dinghy below ground level, he must dig one.

He must dig as close to the sea as he could get, where the cave floor dipped fairly steeply. He could make a hole, put the dinghy into it, get the seal into the dinghy and then dig a channel from the dinghy to the sea's edge. And he must dig where the tide had been. The sand there would be so wet and slippy that the dinghy ought to slide safely and easily into the water.

Before he had finished thinking this out, William had selected the spot and was down on his knees scooping out sand with his bare hands. But this was a painful way of trenching. The sand rasped his skin and dug into his nails. It was slow too.

He looked for a make-shift spade. His eyes picked out the paddles. Just right. He snatched one up and began ploughing out a bath-tub shaped trench. Kneeling on the ground, legs spread apart, he scooped the sand behind him, like a dog digging a hole for a bone.

Very quickly, he excavated a dry dock. Panting, his

arm muscles aching again, he slipped the dinghy into it. The boat fitted snugly, gunwales just a couple of inches below the level of the beach. Exactly as he wanted. But he must hurry now because, even as he watched, water seeped in and the sides of the hole began to crumble. Soon the boat would rise above ground level, floating on a soggy bed of sand.

He ran to the pup, which hissed its warning cry as he approached.

"Can't mess about," William said, breathless. "Got to get you in the boat. Not much time."

This was the moment he had been dreading. Not because he might be bitten, but because he would upset the seal and harm it.

"I don't know!" he said to the pup as he gathered his strength. "Seems to me putting something right can hurt as much as doing something wrong."

He glanced back at the dinghy. Already the gunwales were level with the ground.

"We've got to go," William said. "So look out."

He was talking, he knew, as much to keep up his own courage as to calm the pup.

He rubbed his hands down his jeans to clean them of sand, placed himself behind the pup, and took a deep breath.

He bent, took the pup's two back flippers, one in each of his hands. Their bony fleshiness felt like fingers in skinny gloves.

He dug in his heels and pulled.

The pup slid towards him with such unexpected ease that before William knew what was happening he slumped on to his bottom on the sand, the seal between his spead-eagled legs.

For one shocked second, William and the seal did not move. Then both came to their senses at once.

As William scrambled for safety out of range of its jaws, the pup started thrashing about as hard as it could, churning sand with its front flippers, lashing the ground with its hind ones, while trying at the same time to twist its bulky body so that it could snap at anything in reach. Tears poured from its glorious wide eyes, making trails in the fur of its face; and it screamed as if murder were being done.

"By heck!" William said, laughing despite his anxieties. "A sausage gone berserk!"

Somehow, the pup's exploding anger made it easier for William to do what he must. Moving fast and as firmly as he could, he grasped the seal's hind flippers again and hauled. He knew this time how much weight he had to pull, was prepared for the animal to come slithering towards him.

The pup went on fighting. But its first furious resistance was spent. It tried to dig its fore-flippers into the sand and would have squirmed from William's grasp, but the sand was too dry and loose. William managed to hang on.

"Pack it in," he said between pulls. "You don't want to do circus tricks do you?" He hauled again. "Or be kept for meat..." Another pull. "Or be caged in a zoo..." Pull. "And never go to sea..." Pull. "And never meet other seals..." He was panting again now. "I'm helping you escape..." Pull. Swallow. Deep breath. Pull. "I'm rescuing you..." Pull. "Can't you see that..." Pull. "You ungrateful beast..."

One more effort, the strength draining from his limbs, his hands finding it almost too much to hang on against the seal's tussling, and the pup was lying with its tail end almost against the dinghy's bow.

William let go and sat on the sand. Foolishly, he saw at once. For the seal wanted no rest. It began ploughing its way back up the beach. The sand was firmer here where the tide had been, not soft and loose as it was round the pup's nest. So its flippers found a grip and the seal began land-swimming back to the only home it had ever known.

"Hey, no you don't!" William shouted, scrambling to his feet and grabbing the seal's hind flippers again.

For a moment William and the seal played tug-of-war before he was able to drag the pup back to the boat. This time he held on tight while he caught his breath and took stock.

Getting the pup into the dinghy would be hard enough. But when he got it into the boat, would the pup go on struggling? Would it puncture the boat's plastic skin? Would it be able to push itself out of the dinghy even before they were in the water?

His carefully laid plan seemed full of difficulties he had not foreseen. For the first time, William wished there was someone else there to help him.

The thought reminded him of Gwyn. He glanced at his watch. Twenty minutes after seven. Where had all the time gone! He flushed with panic.

He turned and looked towards the shore. The first thing he saw was the unmistakable figure of Gwyn running along the beach.

No time left for thinking. The seal must take its chance and William with it.

He stood up, still clinging on to the pup's hind flippers, stepped backwards into the dinghy, and pulled the seal gently towards him. A few inches at a time, he dragged the seal off the sand, across the boat's cushioning gunwale and into the boat. There was no room for them both. So as the last of the seal slipped in, William stepped out, and let it go.

The pup fitted neatly inside the dinghy. There was enough room for it to lie comfortably, held by the gunwale, without there being enough space for it to flop about.

William watched to see how the pup took to its new surroundings. Luckily it seemed to like them. Maybe the softness of the inflated plastic pleased it; maybe the strangeness of being in the boat gave it enough to think about. Whatever the reason, the pup stayed calm and quiet.

Hoping it would stay like that for a while, William applied himself to his next problem: digging out a slipway down which he could pull the dinghy and its heavy load into the sea. Using a paddle, he swiftly excavated a channel. As he worked, water seeped into his trench. He was glad: the dinghy would slide more easily.

The channel made, he stood up and stared landward again. Gwyn was still there, peering back at William across the dividing sea. He waved briskly. But he was too far away for William to decide what his signals meant.

Nor did it matter. William had to get the seal away

but he could not go back along the beach. He would have to find a hiding place in the other direction.

William turned back to the dinghy. The pup was warily sniffing out its new resting place. But as soon as William started dragging the boat down the slipway, the pup let out its usual loud hissing snarls, and began banging its flippers on the bottom of the boat so hard William was afraid the plastic skin would burst.

"Oh, pack it in!" he spluttered, his fear finding an outlet in blustering words. But the seal went on thrashing about.

And now the sea faced him, looking suddenly no friend of his. A fresh breeze had sprung up, curling waves on the water, and bringing garbled shouts from Gwyn.

"...ack..." reached him, and a word that sounded like "...ool..."

William paid no attention. Resolutely he walked into the sea towing the boat behind him. The dinghy rode well, was caught by the current and went gliding past William till it was wallowing at the end of its short painter as though wanting to break free.

The pup felt the strange new motion, raised its nose and sniffed the air. Spray fell over it. The seal shook its head like a dog and its whole body started trembling, whether from excitement or fright William could not tell. But he smiled, because he trembled in exactly the same way whenever he was going into the sea for the first time each holiday.

He glanced across the water again. Gwyn was wading into the sea, trying to get across to the cave. But he was already up to his waist so the water must still be too deep. Did that mean it would be too deep in the direction William was taking?

His heart thumped at the thought. He certainly couldn't swim and pull the dinghy at the same time. Even without the boat in tow, he doubted if he could swim far. Not with the sea breaking in choppy little waves and the strong under-surface currents he could feel swirling around his legs. Even where he was standing now waves were rising and falling between his knees and his waist. He wouldn't want to chance them getting higher.

Cautiously William set off, the dinghy's painter wrapped tightly in his left hand, his other arm held out to help keep his balance. He knew he must not cling too closely to the cliff because the sea was breaking white against it. He might get swamped in all that churning foam and sloshing water. But neither dare he go out too far, because the ground might slope away and leave him without a footing.

So he edged seawards, but carefully, searching out each step with his foot to make sure there was firm ground to stand on.

Progress was slow. The dinghy danced about, giving annoying tugs on its painter as the waves tossed it about. William had to work hard to keep himself calm and patient.

But he could not stop that awful memory coming back to him of his father egging him on to take a plunge, and then stepping away when William did as he was told and threw himself towards his father's outstretched arms.

The memory weakened his resolve. He felt his

determination seeping from him. He paused and drew in a deep, sea-tangy breath. The air cooled his burning chest. But his mouth was sour and dry. He was shivering with cold and, he admitted to himself, fear too.

Gwyn, he saw, was back on the beach, and watching. He was shading his eyes with his hand. This time he did not wave or shout. Maybe, William thought ruefully, if he had been patient, he could have talked Gwyn out of his secret plan. That would have been better than this sick-making rescue. And then he would still have had Gwyn to spend his holiday with. Even if he didn't like Gwyn much, it was better to have someone to be with than no one at all.

How he wished he had someone with him now! For a brief moment he thought of turning back, of taking the seal to the cave, and paddling the dinghy across to Gwyn, and trying to explain what had happened and why.

But the next moment he knew this was impossible. Gwyn would never understand. And, William gloomily told himself once more, he had set out to save the seal and he could not give up now, no matter what.

It was then that several things happened at the same time.

William took a step forward. As he did so, the dinghy went surging past him. As if rising to meet the dinghy, a fully-grown seal's head bobbed out of the water a few feet away, like a swimmer taking his bearings.

Both events startled William: the dinghy startled him out of his dark thoughts; and the seal startled him by its sudden and unexpected appearance.

At the same moment the baby seal caught sight of the new arrival, and this sent the pup into a struggling frenzy more violent than anything William had yet witnessed.

William was quite sure the pup would tear the dinghy's skin. So he plunged recklessly towards the dinghy to try and hold it still.

But his feet found nothing but water. Instinctively, William grabbed for the boat. His hands caught the gunwale. He held on for dear life. Frantic, he trod water, trying to touch the bottom, but even with his legs at full stretch and his chin at water level he could not.

All the time the pup was flapping and twisting inside the boat, making the little craft lurch about, so that it was all the harder for William to hang on.

Already the sea felt different: heavier somehow, stronger. And the dinghy was rising and falling in a way that William knew meant it was drifting seawards fast.

Desperate, he pulled himself violently upwards, at the same time thrusting downwards with his legs just as he would to pull himself out of a swimming pool. As he rose out of the water he flung himself across the dinghy's gunwale. He hoped to lie there half in and half out of the dinghy, while he decided what to do.

But he had forgotten that the seal was head-on towards him. As he pulled upwards the dinghy's bow dipped under his weight. The seal slid down, and as William flung himself over the gunwale, the pup snapped with its jaws. It managed to bite him once, firmly on his left arm.

The pain was so sharp William screamed and tore his arm away. He saw blood stream from the wound.

The boat went on tipping into the water. A wave rode by. Water swirled into the dinghy. The seal flapped, caught the surging water, and almost somersaulted itself into the sea.

With the seal's weight thrown out, and the wave passed by, the dinghy bobbed up again, somehow scooping William up with it, so that he found himself tumbling into the dinghy. Instinctively, he hung on with his unhurt hand and managed to keep himself inside.

He was safe. But the seal was gone. Holding his wounded arm close to his body, he sat up and swept the surrounding water with his eyes. The baby seal was not far away, floating low in the water like a soggy seaside toy, only the top of its podgy back showing. The adult seal was not far away, still interestedly watching William and the boat, and paying no heed to the pup. Then a wave that was bigger than most obscured William's view. When it had gone by both seals had disappeared.

William searched again and again for another sight of the pup. But it was gone. The rescue was over.

The Call of the Wild

by Jack London

Once Buck enjoyed the luxury of a fine house, now he is a sledge dog and works in the frozen extremes of Canada. It is a hard life, where only the tough survive. Buck's new owners, Mercedes, Charles and Hal, have little experience of using a pack of huskies, and slowly the dogs' strength diminishes...

With the dogs falling, Mercedes weeping and riding, Hal swearing innocuously, and Charles's eyes wistfully watering, they staggered into John Thornton's camp at the mouth of White River. When they halted, the dogs dropped down as though they had all been struck dead. Mercedes dried her eyes and looked at John Thornton. Charles sat down on a log to rest. He sat down very slowly and painstakingly because of his great stiffness. Hal did the talking. John Thornton was whittling the last touches of an axe-handle he had made from a stick of birch. He whittled and listened, gave monosyllabic replies, and, when it was asked, terse advice. He knew the breed, and he gave his advice in the certainty that it would not be followed.

"They told us up above that the bottom was dropping out of the trail and that the best thing for us to do was to lay over," Hal said in response to Thornton's warning to take no more chances on the rotten ice. "They told us we couldn't make White River, and here we are." This last with a sneering ring of triumph in it.

"And they told you true," John Thornton answered. "The bottom's likely to drop out at any moment. Only fools, with the blind luck of fools, could have made it. I tell you straight, I wouldn't risk my carcass on that ice for all the gold in Alaska."

"That's because you're not a fool, I suppose," said Hal. "All the same, we'll go on to Dawson." He uncoiled his whip. "Get up there, Buck! Hi! Get up there! Mush on!"

Thornton went on whittling. It was idle, he knew, to get between a fool and his folly; while two or three fools more or less would not alter the scheme of things.

But the team did not get up at the command. It had long since passed into the stage where blows were required to rouse it. The whip flashed out, here and there, on its merciless errands. John Thornton compressed his lips. Sol-leks was the first to crawl to his feet. Teek followed. Joe came next, yelping with pain. Pike made painful efforts. Twice he fell over, when half up, and on the third attempt managed to rise. Buck made no effort. He lay quietly where he had fallen. The lash bit into him again and again, but he neither whined nor struggled. Several times Thornton started, as though to speak, but changed his mind. A moisture came into his eyes, and, as the whipping continued, he arose and walked irresolutely up and down.

This was the first time Buck had failed, in itself a sufficient reason to drive Hal into a rage. He exchanged the whip for the customary club. Buck refused to move under the rain of heavier blows which now fell upon him. Like his mates, he was barely able to get up, but, unlike them, he had made up his mind not to get up. He had a vague feeling of impending doom. This had been strong upon him when he pulled in to the bank, and it had not departed from him. What of the thin and rotten ice he had felt under his feet all day, it seemed that he sensed disaster close at hand, out there ahead on the ice where his master was trying to drive him. He refused to stir. So greatly had he suffered, and so far gone was he, that the blows did not hurt much. And as they continued to fall upon him, the spark of life within flickered and went down. It was nearly out. He felt strangely numb. As though from a great distance, he was aware that he was being beaten. The last sensations of pain left him. He no longer felt anything, though very faintly he could hear the impact of the club upon his body. But it was no longer his body, it seemed so far away.

And then, suddenly, without warning, uttering a cry that was inarticulate and more like the cry of an animal, John Thornton sprang upon the man who wielded the club. Hal was hurled backward, as though struck by a falling tree. Mercedes screamed. Charles looked on wistfully, wiping his watery eyes, but did not get up because of his stiffness.

John Thornton stood over Buck, struggling to control himself, too convulsed with rage to speak.

"If you strike that dog again, I'll kill you," he at last managed to say in a choking voice.

"It's my dog," Hal replied, wiping the blood from his mouth as he came back. "Get out of my way, or I'll fix you. I'm going to Dawson."

Thornton stood between him and Buck, and evinced no intention of getting out of the way. Hal drew his long hunting-knife. Mercedes screamed, cried, laughed and manifested the chaotic abandonment of hysteria. Thornton rapped Hal's knuckles with the axe-handle, knocking the knife to the ground. He rapped his knuckles again as he tried to pick it up. Then he stooped, picked it up himself, and with two strokes cut Buck's traces.

Hal had no fight left in him. Besides, his hands were full with his sister, or his arms, rather; while Buck was too near dead to be of further use in hauling the sled. A few minutes later they pulled out from the bank and down the river. Buck heard them go and raised his head to see. Pike was leading, Sol-leks was at the wheel, and between were Joe and Teek. They were limping and staggering. Mercedes was riding the loaded sled. Hal guided at the gee-pole, and Charles stumbled along in the rear.

As Buck watched them, Thornton knelt beside him and with rough, kindly hands searched for broken bones. By the time his search had disclosed nothing more than many bruises and a state of terrible starvation, the sled was a quarter of a mile away. Dog and man watched it crawling along over the ice. Suddenly, they saw its back end drop down, as into a rut, and the gee-pole, with Hal clinging to it, jerk into the air. Mercedes's scream came to their ears. They saw Charles turn and make one step to run back, and then a whole section of ice gave way and dogs and humans disappeared. A yawning hole was all that was to be seen. The bottom had dropped out of the trail.

John Thornton and Buck looked at each other.

"You poor devil," said John Thornton, and Buck licked his hand.

When John Thornton froze his feet in the previous December, his partners had made him comfortable and left him to get well, going on themselves up the river to get out a raft of saw-logs for Dawson. He was still limping slightly at the time he rescued Buck, but with the continued warm weather even the slight limp left him. And here, lying by the river bank through the long spring days, watching the running water, listening lazily to the songs of birds and the hum of nature, Buck slowly won back his strength.

A rest comes very good after one has travelled three thousand miles, and it must be confessed that Buck waxed lazy as his wounds healed, his muscles swelled out, and the flesh came back to cover his bones. For that matter, they were all loafing – Buck, John Thornton, and Skeet and Nig – waiting for the raft to come that was to carry them down to Dawson. Skeet was a little Irish setter who early made friends with Buck, who, in a dying condition, was unable to resent her first advances. She had the doctor trait which some dogs possess; and as a mother cat washes her kittens, so she washed and cleansed Buck's wounds. Regularly, each morning, after he had finished his breakfast, she performed her self-appointed task, till he came to look for her ministrations as much as he did for Thornton's. Nig, equally friendly, though less demonstrative, was a huge black dog, half bloodhound and half deerhound, with eyes that laughed and a boundless good nature.

To Buck's surprise these dogs manifested no jealously toward him. They seemed to share the kindliness and largeness of John Thornton. As Buck grew stronger they enticed him into all sorts of ridiculous games, in which Thornton himself could not forbear to join; and in this fashion Buck romped through his convalescence and into a new existence. Love, genuine passionate love, was his for the first time. This he had never experienced at Judge Miller's down in the sun-kissed Santa Clara Valley. With the Judge's son, hunting and tramping, it had been a working partnership; with the Judge's grandsons, a sort of pompous guardianship; and with the Judge himself, a stately and dignified friendship. But love that was feverish and burning, that was adoration, that was madness, it had taken John Thornton to arouse.

This man had saved his life, which was something; but, further, he was the ideal master. Other men saw to the welfare of their dogs from a sense of duty and business expediency; he saw to the welfare of his as if they were his own children, because he could not help it. And he saw further. He never forgot a kindly greeting or a cheering word, and to sit down for a long talk with them ("gas" he called it) was as much his delight as theirs. He had a way of taking Buck's head roughly between his hands, and resting his own head upon Buck's, of shaking him back and forth, the while calling him ill names that to Buck were love names. Buck knew no greater joy than that rough embrace and the sound of murmured oaths, and at each jerk back and forth it seemed that his heart would be shaken out of his body so great was its ecstasy. And when, released, he sprang to his feet, his mouth laughing, his eyes eloquent, his throat vibrant with unuttered sounds, and in that fashion remained without movement, John Thornton would reverently exclaim, "God, you can all but speak!"

Buck had a trick of love expression that was akin to hurt. He would often seize Thornton's hand in his mouth and close so fiercely that the flesh bore impress of his teeth for some time afterwards. And as Buck understood the oaths to be love words, so the man understood this feigned bite for a caress.

For the most part, however, Buck's love was expressed in adoration. While he went wild with happiness when Thornton touched him or spoke to him, he did not seek these tokens. Unlike Skeet, who was wont to shove her nose under Thornton's hand and nudge and nudge till petted, or Nig, who would stalk up and rest his great head on Thornton's knee, Buck was content to adore at a distance. He would lie by the hour, eager, alert, at Thornton's feet looking up into his face, dwelling upon it, studying it, following with keenest interest each fleeting expression, every movement or change of feature. Or, as chance might have it, he would lie farther away, to the side or rear, watching the outlines of the man and the occasional movements of his body. And often, such was the communion in which they lived, the strength of Buck's gaze would draw John Thornton's head around, and he would return the gaze, without speech, his heart shining out of his eyes as Buck's heart shone out.

For a long time after his rescue, Buck did not like Thornton to get out of his sight. From the moment he left the tent to when he entered it again, Buck would follow at his heels. His transient masters since he had come into the Northland had bred in him a fear that no master could be permanent. He was afraid that Thornton would pass out of his life as Perrault and Francois and the Scotch half-breed had passed out. Even in the night, in his dreams, he was haunted by this fear. At such times he would shake off sleep and creep through the chill to the flap of the tent, where he would stand and listen to the sound of his master's breathing.

But in spite of this great love he bore John Thornton, which seemed to bespeak the soft civilizing influence, the strain of the primitive, which the Northland had aroused in him, remained alive and active. Faithfulness and devotion, things born of fire and roof, were his, yet he retained his wildness and wiliness. He was a thing of the wild, come in from the wild to sit by John Thornton's fire, rather than a dog of the soft Southland stamped with the marks of generations of civilization. Because of his very great love, he could not steal from this man, but from any man, in any other camp, he did not hesitate an instant; while the cunning with which he stole enabled him to escape detection.

His face and body were scored by the teeth of many dogs, and he fought as fiercely as ever and more shrewdly. Skeet and Nig were too good-natured for quarrelling – besides, they belonged to John Thornton; but the strange dog, no matter what the breed or valour, swiftly acknowledged Buck's supremacy or found himself struggling for life with a terrible antagonist. And Buck was merciless. He had learned well the law of club and fang, and he never forwent an advantage or drew back from a foe he had started on the way to Death. He had lessoned from Spitz, and from the chief fighting dogs of the police and mail, and knew there was no middle course. He must master or be mastered; while to show mercy was a weakness. Mercy did not exist in the primordial life. It was misunderstood for fear, and such misunderstandings made for death. Kill or be killed, eat or be eaten, was the law; and this mandate, handed down out of the depths of Time, he obeyed.

He was older than the days he had seen and the breaths he had drawn. He linked the past with the present, and the eternity behind him throbbed through him in a mighty rhythm to which he swayed as the tides and seasons swayed. He sat by John Thornton's fire, a broad-breasted dog, white-fanged and long-furred; but behind him were the shades of all manner of dogs, half-wolves and wild wolves, urgent and prompting, tasting the savour of the meat he ate, thirsting for the water he drank, scenting the wind with him, listening with him and telling him the sounds made by the wild life in the forest, dictating his moods, directing his actions, lying down to sleep with him when he lay down, and dreaming with him and beyond him and becoming themselves the stuff of his dreams.

So peremptorily did these shades beckon him, that each day mankind and the claims of mankind slipped farther from him. Deep in the forest a call was sounding, and as often as he heard this call, mysteriously thrilling and luring, he felt compelled to turn his back upon the fire and the beaten earth around it, and to plunge into the forest, and on and on, he knew not where or why; nor did he wonder where or why, the call sounding imperiously, deep in the forest. But as often as he gained the soft unbroken earth and the green shade, the love for John Thornton drew him back to the fire again.

Thornton alone held him. The rest of mankind was as nothing. Chance travellers might praise or pet him; but he was cold under it all, and from a too demonstrative man he would get up and walk away. When Thornton's partners, Hans and Pete, arrived on the long-expected raft Buck refused to notice them till he learned they were close to Thornton; after that he tolerated them in a passive sort of way, accepting favours from them as though he favoured them by accepting. They were of the same large type as Thornton, living close to the earth, thinking simply and seeing clearly; and ere they swung the raft into the big eddy by the sawmill at Dawson, they understood Buck and his ways, and did not insist upon an intimacy such as obtained with Skeet and Nig.

For Thornton, however, his love seemed to grow and grow. He, alone among men, could put a pack upon Buck's back in the summer travelling. Nothing was too great for Buck to do, when Thornton commanded. One day (they had grub-staked themselves from the proceeds of the raft and left Dawson for the head-waters of the Tanana), the men and dogs were sitting on the crest of a cliff which fell away, straight down, to naked bed-rock three hundred feet below. John Thornton was sitting near the edge, Buck at his shoulder. A thoughtless whim seized Thornton, and he drew the attention of Hans and Pete to the experiment he had in mind. "Jump, Buck!" he commanded, sweeping his arm out and over the chasm. The next instant he was grappling with Buck on the extreme edge, while Hans and Pete were dragging them back into safety.

"It's uncanny," Pete said, after it was over and they caught their speech.

Thornton shook his head. "No, it is splendid, and it is terrible too. Do you know, it sometimes makes me afraid."

"I'm not hankering to be the man that lays hands on you while he's around," Pete announced conclusively, nodding his head toward Buck.

"By Jingo!" was Hans' contribution. "Not mineself either."

It was at Circle City, ere the year was out, that Pete's apprehensions were realised. 'Black' Burton, a man evil-tempered and malicious, had been picking a quarrel with a tenderfoot at the bar, when Thornton stepped good-naturedly between. Buck, as was his custom, was lying in a corner, head on paws, watching his master's every action. Burton struck out, without warning, straight from the shoulder. Thornton was sent spinning, and saved himself from falling only by clutching the rail of the bar.

Those who were looking on heard what was neither bark nor yelp, but a something which is best described as a roar, and they saw Buck's body rise up in the air as

102

he left the floor for Burton's throat. The man saved his life by instinctively throwing out his arm, but was hurled backward to the floor with Buck on top of him. Buck loosed his teeth from the flesh of the arm and drove in again for the throat. This time the man succeeded only in partly blocking, and his throat was torn open. Then the crowd was upon Buck, and he was driven off; but while a surgeon checked the bleeding, he prowled up and down, growling furiously, attempting to rush in, and being forced back by an array of hostile clubs. A 'miners' meeting', called on the spot, decided that the dog had sufficient provocation, and Buck was discharged. But his reputation was made, and from that day his name spread through every camp in Alaska.

Later on, in the fall of the year, he saved John Thornton's life in quite another fashion. The three partners were lining a long and narrow poling-boat down a bad stretch of rapids on the Forty-Mile Creek. Hans and Pete moved along the bank, snubbing with a thin Manila rope from tree to tree, while Thornton remained in the boat, helping the descent by means of a pole, and shouting directions to the shore. Buck, on the bank, worried and anxious, kept abreast of the boat, his eyes never off his master.

At a particularly bad spot where a ledge of barely submerged rocks jutted out into the river, Hans cast off the rope, and, while Thornton poled the boat out into the stream, ran down the bank with the end in his hand to snub the boat when it had cleared the ledge. This it did, and was flying downstream in a current as swift as a mill-race, when Hans checked it with the rope and checked too suddenly. The boat flirted over and snubbed into the bank bottom up, while Thornton, flung sheer out of it, was carried downstream toward the worst part of the rapids, a stretch of wild water in which no swimmer could live.

Buck had sprung in on the instant; and at the end of three hundred yards, amid a mad swirl of water, he overhauled Thornton. When he felt him grasp his tail, Buck headed for the bank, swimming with all his splendid strength. But the progress shoreward was slow; the progress downstream amazingly rapid. From below came the fatal roaring where the wild current went wilder and was rent in shreds and spray by the rocks which thrust through like the teeth of an enormous comb. The suck of the water as it took the beginning of the last steep pitch was frightful, and Thornton knew that the shore was impossible. He scraped furiously over a rock, bruised across a second, and struck a third with crushing force. He clutched its slippery top with both hands, releasing Buck, and above the roar of the churning water shouted: "Go, Buck! Go!"

Buck could not hold his own, and swept on downstream, struggling desperately, but unable to win back. When he heard Thornton's command repeated, he partly reared out of the water, throwing his head high as though for a last look, then turned obediently toward the bank. He swam powerfully and was dragged ashore by Pete and Hans at the very point where swimming ceased to be possible and destruction began.

They knew that the time a man could cling to a slippery rock in the face of that driving current was a matter of minutes, and they ran as fast as they could up the bank to a point far above where Thornton was hanging on. They attached the line with which they had been snubbing the boat to Buck's neck and shoulders, being careful that it should neither strangle him nor impede his swimming and launched him into the stream. He struck out boldly but not straight enough into the stream. He discovered the mistake too late, when Thornton was abreast of him and a bare half-dozen strokes away while he was being carried helplessly past.

Hans promptly snubbed with the rope, as though Buck were a boat. The rope thus tightening on him in the sweep of the current, he was jerked under the surface, and under the surface he remained till his body struck against the bank and he was hauled out. He was half drowned, and Hans and Pete threw themselves upon him, pounding the breath into him and the water out of him. He staggered to his feet and fell down. The faint sound of Thornton's voice came to them, and though they could not make out the words of it, they knew that he was in his extremity. His master's voice acted on Buck like an electric shock. He sprang to his feet and ran up the bank ahead of the men to the point of his previous departure.

Again the rope was attached and he was launched, and again he struck out, but this time straight into the stream. He had miscalculated once, but he would not be guilty of it a second time. Hans paid out the rope, permitting no slack, while Pete kept it clear of coils. Buck held on till he was on a line straight above Thornton; then he turned, and with the speed of an express train headed down upon him. Thornton saw him coming, and, as Buck struck him like a battering ram, with the whole force of the current behind him, he reached up and closed with both arms around the shaggy neck. Hans snubbed the rope around the tree, and Buck and Thornton were jerked under the water. Strangling, suffocating, sometimes one uppermost and sometimes the other, dragging over the jagged bottom, smashing against rocks and snags, they veered in to the bank.

Thornton came to, belly downward and being violently propelled back and forth across a drift log by Hans and Pete. His first glance was for Buck, over whose limp and apparently lifeless body Nig was setting up a howl, while Skeet was licking the wet face and closed eyes. Thornton was himself bruised and battered, and he went carefully over Buck's body, when he had been brought around, finding three broken ribs.

"That settles it," he announced. "We camp right here." And camp they did, till Buck's ribs knitted and he was able to travel.

That winter, at Dawson, Buck performed another exploit, not so heroic, perhaps, but one that put his name many notches higher on the totem-pole of Alaskan fame. This exploit was particularly gratifying to the three men; for they stood in need of the outfit which it furnished, and were enabled to make a long-desired trip into the virgin East, where miners had not yet appeared. It was brought about by a conversation in the Eldorado Saloon, in which men waxed boastful of their favourite dogs. Buck, because of his record, was the target of these men, and Thornton was driven stoutly to defend him. At the end of half an hour one man stated that his dog could start a sled with five hundred pounds and walk off with it; a second bragged six hundred for his dog; and a third, seven hundred.

"Pooh! pooh!" said John Thornton; "Buck can start a thousand pounds."

"And break it out? And walk off with it for a hundred yards?" demanded Matthewson, a Bonanza King, he of the seven hundred vaunt.

"And break it out, and walk off with it for a hundred yards," John Thornton said coolly.

"Well," Matthewson said, slowly and deliberately, so that all could hear, "I've got a thousand dollars that says he can't. And there it is." So saying, he slammed a sack of gold dust of the size of a bologna sausage down upon the bar.

Nobody spoke. Thornton's bluff, if bluff it was, had been called. He could feel a flush of warm blood creeping up his face. His tongue had tricked him. He did not know whether Buck could start a thousand pounds. Half a ton! The enormousness of it appalled him. He had great faith in Buck's strength and had often thought him capable of starting such a load; but never, as now, had he faced the possibility of it, the eyes of a dozen men fixed upon him, silent and waiting. Further, he had no thousand dollars; nor had Hans or Pete.

"I've got a sled standing outside now, with twenty fifty-pound sacks of flour on it," Matthewson went on, with brutal directness, "so don't let that hinder you."

Thornton did not reply. He did not know what to say. He glanced from face to face in the absent way of a man who has lost the power of thought and is seeking

107

somewhere to find the thing that will start it going again. The face of Jim O'Brien, a Mastodon King and old-time comrade, caught his eyes. It was a cue to him, seeming to rouse him to do what he would never have dreamed of doing.

"Can you lend me a thousand?" he asked, almost in a whisper.

"Sure," answered O'Brien, thumping down a plethoric sack by the side of Matthewson's. "Though it's little faith I'm having, John, that the beast can do the trick."

The Eldorado emptied its occupants into the street to see the test. The tables were deserted, and the dealers and gamekeepers came forth to see the outcome of the wager and to lay odds. Several hundred men, furred and mittened, banked around the sled within easy distance. Matthewson's sled, loaded with a thousand pounds of flour, had been standing for a couple of hours, and in the intense cold (it was sixty below zero) the runners had frozen fast to the hard-packed snow. Men offered odds of two to one that Buck could not budge the sled. A quibble arose concerning the phrase 'break out'. O'Brien contended it was Thornton's privilege to knock the runners loose, leaving Buck to 'break it out' from a dead standstill. Matthewson insisted that the phrase included breaking the runners from the frozen grip of the snow. A majority of the men who had witnessed the making of the bet decided in his favour, whereat the odds went up to three to one against Buck.

There were no takers. Not a man believed him capable of the feat. Thornton had been hurried into the wager, heavy with doubt, and now that he looked at the sled itself, the concrete fact, with the regular team of ten dogs curled up on the snow before it, the more impossible the task appeared. Matthewson waxed jubilant.

"Three to one!" he proclaimed. "I'll lay you another thousand at that figure, Thornton. What d'ye say?"

Thornton's doubt was strong in his face, but his fighting spirit was aroused – the fighting spirit that soars above odds, fails to recognise the impossible, and is deaf to all save the clamour for battle. He called Hans and Pete to him. Their sacks were slim, and with his own the three partners could rake together only two hundred dollars. In the ebb of their fortunes, this sum was their total capital; yet they laid it unhesitatingly against Matthewson's six hundred.

The team of ten dogs was unhitched, and Buck, with his own harness, was put into the sled. He had caught the contagion of the excitement, and he felt that in some way he must do a great thing for John Thornton. Murmurs of admiration at his splendid condition, without an ounce of superfluous flesh, and the one hundred and fifty pounds that he weighed were so many pounds of grit and virility. His furry coat shone with the sheen of silk. Down the neck and across the shoulders, his mane, in repose as it was, half bristled and seemed to lift with every movement, as though excess of vigour made each particular hair alive and active. The great breast and heavy fore legs were no more than in proportion with the rest of the body, where the muscles showed in tight rolls underneath the skin. Men felt these muscles and proclaimed them hard as iron, and the odds went down to two to one.

"Gad, sir! Gad, sir!" stuttered a member of the latest dynasty, a king of the Skookum Benches. "I offer you eight hundred for him, sir, before the test, sir; eight hundred just as he stands."

Thornton shook his head and stepped to Buck's side.

"You must stand off from him," Matthewson protested. "Free play and plenty of room."

The crowd fell silent; only could be heard the voices of the gamblers vainly offering two to one. Everybody acknowledged Buck a magnificent animal, but twenty fifty-pound sacks of flour bulked too large in their eyes for them to loosen their pouch-strings.

Thornton knelt down by Buck's side. He took his head in his two hands and rested cheek on cheek. He did not playfully shake him, as was his wont, or murmur soft love curses; but he whispered in his ear. "As you love me, Buck. As you love me," was what he whispered. Buck whined with suppressed eagerness.

The crowd was watching curiously. The affair was growing mysterious. It seemed like a conjuration. As Thornton got to his feet, Buck seized his mittened hand between his jaws, pressing in with his teeth and releasing slowly, half-reluctantly. It was the answer, in terms, not of speech, but of love. Thornton stepped well back.

"Now, Buck," he said.

Buck tightened the traces, then slacked them for a matter of several inches. It was the way he had learned.

"Gee!" Thornton's voice rang out, sharp in the tense silence.

Buck swung to the right, ending the movement in a

110

plunge that took up the slack and with a sudden jerk arrested his one hundred and fifty pounds. The load quivered, and from under the runners arose a crisp crackling.

"Haw!" Thornton commanded.

Buck duplicated the manoeuvre, this time to the left. The crackling turning into a snapping, the sled pivoting and the runners slipping and grating several inches to the side. The sled was broken out. Men were holding their breaths, intensely unconscious of the fact.

"Now, MUSH!"

Thornton's command cracked out like a pistol-shot. Buck threw himself forward, tightening the traces with a jarring lunge. His whole body was gathered compactly together in the tremendous effort, the muscles writhing and knotting like live things under the silky fur. His great chest was low to the ground, his head forward and down, while his feet were flying like mad, the claws scarring the hard-packed snow in parallel grooves. The sled swayed and trembled, half-started forward. One of his feet slipped, and one man groaned aloud. Then the sled lurched ahead in what appeared a rapid succession of jerks, though it never really came to a dead stop again... half an inch... an inch... two inches... The jerks perceptibly diminished; as the sled gained momentum, he caught them up, till it was moving steadily along.

Men gasped and began to breathe again, unaware that for a moment they had ceased to breathe. Thornton was running behind, encouraging Buck with short, cheery words. The distance had been measured off, and as he neared the pile of firewood which marked the end of the hundred yards, a cheer began to grow and grow, which burst into a roar as he passed the firewood and halted at command. Every man was tearing himself loose, even Matthewson. Hats and mittens were flying in the air. Men were shaking hands, it did not matter with whom, and bubbling over in a general incoherent babel.

But Thornton fell on his knees beside Buck. Head was against head, and he was shaking him back and forth. Those who hurried up heard him cursing Buck and he cursed long and fervently, and softly and lovingly.

Silly Old Moo

Michael Morpurgo

I knew I should have gone for help, but I wanted to do it by myself, on my own. I'd seen it done often enough. After all, I'd spent all of my nine years growing up on a dairy farm. I could do it – or that's what I thought.

I was coming up from the river. I'm always down there watching for otters and herons and kingfishers, but all I'd seen that day was a pair of mallard ducks. It was a late summer's evening and I was hungry for my tea. I'd just climbed Long Meadow gate when I noticed Blossom lying down by the hedge. I saw her rocking over onto her side. She was calving. I wasn't surprised. We'd been expecting it for a day or so. I could see already there were two white feet showing under her lifted tail, and as I came closer she was pushing, and pushing hard.

I remember what Dad had told me: "Nine times out of ten, they're better off doing it on their own, Josh. Just let them get on with it." So I crouched down and waited and watched, and let her get on with it. I kept telling myself I should go and find Dad and let him know, just in case things went on for too long, just in case things went wrong. But then I'd think: "No. I don't need Dad.

I know what to do. I'll do it on my own. I'll manage."

All the while – and it seemed like hours – Blossom bellowed in her pain, and ground her teeth and swished her tail. Then, unsettled and upset, she got up and moved away from me along the hedgerow. I didn't follow at once, but crouched where I was and waited for her to lie down again, which at long last she did with a great groan of resignation. She wanted it over with – I could see it in her eyes. She'd had enough. After all that effort, all that suffering, the calf's feet were still no further out, and I could see no sign of a head. She was in trouble. She wanted my help, she needed me.

I went over to her and knelt beside her. I talked to her and stroked her neck, to reassure her, to calm her. It's what Dad always did. She gave a sudden strident bellow, a dreadful strangulated cry, that echoed across the valley, and inside my head. I would have to do it, and do it now. I mustn't wait any longer. I went around behind her, talking as I went. "There's a good girl. You'll be all right, Blossom. We'll do it together, you and me. You push, I'll pull. It'll soon be over, you'll see."

Just for a moment I thought of running back to the barn for calving ropes, to tie on each foot – I'd be able to pull better with the ropes. But I didn't like to leave her, not now; and besides, Dad might see me, and then I wouldn't be able to do it on my own. I'd have to manage without ropes. Dad didn't always use the ropes.

I crouched down behind her rump and cleared away the clinging membrane. I could see a black tongue now, half in, half out, between the two white feet, and had just a glimpse of a nose. "She's coming, Blossom," I told her. "She's coming. Keep pushing. Keep pushing."

I took a foot in each hand, braced myself and made ready to pull. But the feet were slimy. I couldn't get a proper grip. I tried wiping them clean with handfuls of grass, but my hands kept slipping every time I took the strain.

It was as I was rubbing my hands dry that I had an idea. I took off my shirt, wrapped it around both legs, grasped them tight, and waited for the next groaning push, and then pulled with her. I pulled as Dad had taught me to pull, gently at first, then harder, always in rhythm with the pushing. But I was getting nowhere. For all my huffing and puffing, the calf hardly budged – still only two feet and a tongue and a nose. Whatever progress we made when Blossom pushed was lost when she relaxed. As she lay there recovering from each great surging effort, it seemed as if she was sucking the calf back inside her, as if she didn't want it to be born at all.

I kept saying to myself – one last pull and I'll go for help, but I never did. I had been pulling for so long now, and so hard, that my arms felt as if they were coming out of their sockets. I knew I just hadn't the strength to go on much longer. I gave one last desperate heave, and the nose suddenly came clear. I saw the eyes, dark blue, and they were looking at me, begging me to go on. A few more heaves and the whole head slipped out. The rest would follow easily enough I thought. But it didn't. For some reason Blossom seemed to think it was all over. She simply stopped pushing. I yelled at her and yelled at her, and just kept on pulling. I knew full well the calf would die if I couldn't pull her out soon. Too late now to go for Dad. I screamed at Blossom to get on with it, and hauled on the feet with all my might. I felt

115

her push with me, and then in one slide, in one great whoosh of blood and membrane the calf came free, flopping down on the grass at my feet. Black and beautiful she was, and steaming in the evening air. I'd done it! I'd done it all by myself.

Blossom didn't get up to lick the calf. That didn't worry me – cows often lie there for a while afterwards, to get their strength back. She was breathing hard, every now and again mooing contentedly. She knew the job was over and done. She seemed relieved, pleased with herself, proud of her calf, happy. And then I noticed the calf was still. Quite still. Too still. She wasn't shaking her head. She wasn't breathing. Her eyes were closed. I knelt over her and put my ear to her nose. No breath. Not a sign of life.

Panic gripped me at once. I leapt to my feet and ran. I ran home that evening faster than I'd ever run in my life. Dad was sitting over his tea in the kitchen when I burst in bloodied and bare chested. "Blossom's calf. I think I've killed her," I cried. "She won't breathe! She won't breathe!"

We took the pick-up. I jumped in the back and hung on as we rattled and bumped across the field. Blossom was sitting where I'd left her, the calf stretched out nearby. By the time I was out of the pick-up Dad was already on his knees beside the calf. He had his ear to her chest, listening for the heartbeat. I could hear my own pounding in my ears.

"She's alive," Dad said, "but only just. Straw, Josh, fetch me some straw. It's in the back of the pick-up. Just a handful." I dashed to the pick-up. By the time I got back, Dad was giving the calf mouth to mouth

116

resuscitation. But still the calf would not breathe. He rubbed her vigorously all over, took her by the legs, shook her, turned her over, rubbed her again and then gave her more mouth to mouth. All the while the calf lay there still as death.

"You got that straw?" Dad asked. I handed it to him. He took just one long stalk of it, and wriggled it up the calf's nostril, first one then the other. "Breathe my beauty," he whispered. "Breathe!"

The calf gave a sudden snort, snuffled, coughed, and took a breath. Her eyes were open! She lifted her head and shook it. Dad laughed, sitting back on his haunches. "There we are. Alive, alive-o." He got to his feet and put his arm around me. "You did well, Josh," he said. "Big calf, too. Good thing you came along when

117

you did. That calf might have died if you hadn't been there to give a hand. Proper farmer you are. Well done."

But I didn't have time to feel all glowing and good. Suddenly Blossom shifted her great bulk and lurched up onto her feet. She bent over her calf lowing lovingly, licking her all over her face. She looked up at us, and mooed just once, very loudly. I could sense this wasn't a thank you sort of a moo, but until she tossed her head and roared and began to charge at us, I didn't really get the message.

"Run!" Dad shouted, grabbing my arm. I didn't argue. We ran for it. We ran the full length of the field, Blossom behind us all the way. Dad vaulted the gate and hauled me over. Blossom stood there snorting at us like a bull, tossing her head and showing us the whites of her eyes.

"I don't know," said Dad, still breathless. "Between us we saved her calf's life, and that's all the thanks we get. Silly old moo."

The Jungle Book

by Rudyard Kipling

As an infant Mowgli is rescued from the tiger, Shere Khan, and adopted by a wolf pack. Mowgli grows up according to the laws of the jungle, but Shere Khan turns the young wolves against him and drives him from the jungle. As he leaves, Mowgli swears revenge...

What of the hunting, hunter bold?
Brother, the watch was long and cold.
What of the quarry ye went to kill?
Brother, he crops in the Jungle still.
Where is the power that made your pride?
Brother, it ebbs from my flank and side.
Where is the haste that ye hurry by?
Brother, I go to my lair – to die!

Now we must go back to the first tale. When Mowgli left the wolf's cave after the fight with the Pack at the Council Rock, he went down to the ploughed lands where the villagers lived, but he would not stop there because it was too near to the Jungle, and he knew that he had made at least one bad enemy at the Council. So

119

he hurried on, keeping to the rough road that ran down the valley, and followed it at a steady jog-trot for nearly twenty miles, till he came to a country that he did not know. The valley opened out into a great plain dotted over with rocks and cut up by ravines. At one end stood a little village, and at the other the thick Jungle came down in a sweep to the grazing-grounds, and stopped there as though it had been cut off with a hoe. All over the plain, cattle and buffaloes were grazing, and when the little boys in charge of the herds saw Mowgli they shouted and ran away, and the yellow pariah dogs that hang about every Indian village barked. Mowgli walked on, for he was feeling hungry, and when he came to the village gate he saw the big thorn-bush that was drawn up before the gate at twilight pushed to one side.

"Umph!" he said, for he had come across more than one such barricade in his night rambles after things to eat. "So men are afraid of the People of the Jungle here also." He sat down by the gate, and when a man came out he stood up, opened his mouth, and pointed down it to show that he wanted food. The man stared, and ran back up the one street of the village shouting for the priest, who was a big, fat man dressed in white, with a red-and-yellow mark on his forehead. The priest came to the gate, and with him at least a hundred people, who stared and talked and shouted and pointed at Mowgli.

"They have no manners, these Men-Folk," said Mowgli to himself. "Only the grey ape would behave as they do." So he threw back his long hair and frowned at the crowd.

"What is there to be afraid of?" said the priest.

"Look at the marks on his arms and legs. They are the bites of wolves. He is but a wolf-child run away from the Jungle."

Of course, in playing together, the cubs had often nipped Mowgli harder than they intended, and there were white scars all over his arms and legs. But he would have been the last person in the world to call these bites, for he knew what real biting meant.

"Arré! *Arré*!" said two or three women together. "To be bitten by wolves, poor child! He is a handsome boy. He has eyes like red fire. By my honour, Messua, he is not unlike thy boy that was taken by the tiger."

"Let me look," said a woman with heavy copper rings on her wrists and ankles, and she peered at Mowgli under the palm of her hand. "Indeed he is not. He is thinner, but he has the very look of my boy."

The priest was a clever man, and he knew that Messua was wife to the richest villager in the place. So he looked up at the sky for a minute, and said solemnly: "What the Jungle has taken the Jungle has restored. Take the boy into thy house, my sister, and forget not to honour the priest who sees so far into the lives of men."

"By the Bull that bought me," said Mowgli to himself, "but all this talking is like another looking-over by the Pack! Well, if I am a man, a man I must become."

The crowd parted as the woman beckoned Mowgli to her hut, where there was a red-lacquered bedstead, a great earthen grain-chest with curious raised patterns on it, half a dozen copper cooking-pots, an image of a Hindu god in a little alcove, and on the wall a real looking-glass, such as they sell at the country fairs.

She gave him a long drink of milk and some bread,

and then she laid her hand on his head and looked into his eyes; for she thought that perhaps he might be her real son come back from the Jungle where the tiger had taken him. So she said: "Nathoo, O Nathoo!" Mowgli did not show that he knew the name. "Dost thou not remember the day when I gave thee thy new shoes?" She touched his foot, and it was almost as hard as horn. "No," she said sorrowfully, "those feet have never worn shoes, but thou art very like my Nathoo, and thou shalt be my son."

Mowgli was uneasy, because he had never been under a roof before; but as he looked at the thatch, he saw that he could tear it out any time if he wanted to get away, and that the window had no fastenings. "What is the good of a man," he said to himself at last, "if he does not understand man's talk? Now I am as silly and dumb as a man would be with us in the Jungle. I must learn their talk."

It was not for fun that he had learned while he was with the wolves to imitate the challenge of bucks in the Jungle and the grunt of the little wild pig. So as soon as Messua pronounced a word Mowgli would imitate it almost perfectly, and before dark he had learned the names of many things in the hut.

There was a difficulty at bedtime, because Mowgli would not sleep under anything that looked so like a panther-trap as that hut, and when they shut the door he went through the window. "Give him his will," said Messua's husband. "Remember he can never till now have slept on a bed. If he is indeed sent in the place of our son he will not run away."

So Mowgli stretched himself in some long, clean

grass at the edge of the field, but before he had closed his eyes a soft grey nose poked him under the chin.

"Phew!" said Grey Brother (he was the eldest of Mother Wolf's cubs). "This is a poor reward for following thee twenty miles. Thou smellest of wood-smoke and cattle – altogether like a man already. Wake, Little Brother; I bring news."

"Are all well in the Jungle?" said Mowgli, hugging him.

"All except the wolves that were burned with the Red Flower. Now, listen. Shere Khan has gone away to hunt far off till his coat grows again, for he is badly singed. When he returns he swears that he will lay thy bones in the Waingunga."

"There are two words to that. I also have made a little promise. But news is always good. I am tired tonight – very tired with new things, Grey Brother – but bring me the news always."

"Thou wilt not forget that thou art a wolf? Men will not make thee forget?" said Grey Brother anxiously.

"Never. I will always remember that I love thee and all in our cave; but also I will always remember that I have been cast out of the Pack."

"And that thou mayest be cast out of another pack. Men are only men, Little Brother, and their talk is like the talk of frogs in a pond. When I come down here again, I will wait for thee in the bamboos at the edge of the grazing-ground."

For three months after that night Mowgli hardly ever left the village gate, he was so busy learning the ways and customs of men. First he had to wear a cloth round him, which annoyed him horribly; and then he had to learn about money, which he did not in the least understand, and about ploughing, of which he did not see the use. Then the little children in the village made him very angry. Luckily, the Law of the Jungle had taught him to keep his temper, for in the Jungle life and food depend on keeping your temper; but when they made fun of him because he would not play games or fly kites, or because he mispronounced some word, only the knowledge that it was unsportsmanlike to kill little naked cubs kept him from picking them up and breaking them in two.

He did not know his own strength in the least. In the Jungle he knew he was weak compared with the beasts, but in the village people said that he was as strong as a bull.

And Mowgli had not the faintest idea of the difference that caste makes between man and man. When the potter's donkey slipped in the clay-pit, Mowgli hauled it out by the tail, and helped to stack the pots for their journey to the market at Khanhiwara. That was very shocking, too, for the potter is a low-caste man, and his donkey is worse. When the priest scolded him, Mowgli threatened to put him on the donkey, too, and the priest told Messua's husband that Mowgli had better be set to work as soon as possible; and the village headman told Mowgli that he would have to go out with the buffaloes next day, and herd them while they grazed. No one was more pleased than Mowgli; and that night because he had been appointed, as it were, a servant of the village, he went off to a circle that met every evening on a masonry platform under a great fig-tree. It was the village club, and the head-man and the watchman and the barber (who knew all the gossip of the village), and old Buldeo, the village hunter, who owned a Tower musket, met and smoked. The monkeys sat and talked in the upper branches, and there was a hole under the platform where a cobra lived, and he had his little platter of milk every night because he was sacred; and the old men sat around the tree and talked, and pulled at the big hookahs [waterpipes], till far into the night. They told wonderful tales of gods and men and ghosts; and Buldeo told even more wonderful ones of the ways of beasts in the Jungle, till the eyes of the children sitting outside the circle bulged out of their heads. Most of the tales were about animals, for the Jungle was always at their door. The deer and the wild pig grubbed up their crops, and now and again the tiger carried off a man at twilight, within sight of the village gates.

Mowgli, who, naturally, knew something about what they were talking of, had to cover his face not to show that he was laughing, while Buldeo, the Tower musket across his knees, climbed on from one wonderful story to another, and Mowgli's shoulders shook.

Buldeo was explaining how the tiger that had carried away Messua's son was a ghost-tiger, and his body was inhabited by the ghost of a wicked old money-lender, who had died some years ago. "And I know that this is true," he said, "because Purun Dass always limped from the blow that he got in a riot when his account-books were burned, and the tiger that I speak of, *he* limps, too, for the tracks of his pads are unequal."

"True, true; that must be the truth," said the greybeards, nodding together.

"Are all these tales such cobwebs and moontalk?" said Mowgli. "That tiger limps because he was born lame, as every one knows. To talk of the soul of a money-lender in a beast that never had the courage of a jackal is child's talk."

Buldeo was speechless with surprise for a moment, and the head-man stared.

"Oho! It is the Jungle brat, is it?" said Buldeo. "If thou art so wise, better bring his hide to Khanhiwara, for the Government has set a hundred rupees on his life. Better still, do not talk when thy elders speak."

Mowgli rose to go. "All the evening I have lain here listening," he called back over his shoulder, "and, except once or twice, Buldeo has not said one word of truth concerning the Jungle, which is at his very doors. How, then, shall I believe the tales of ghosts and gods and goblins which he says he has seen?"

"It is full time that boy went to herding," said the head-man, while Buldeo puffed and snorted at Mowgli's impertinence.

The custom of most Indian villages is for a few boys to take the cattle and buffaloes out to graze in the early morning, and bring them back at night; and the very cattle that would trample a white man to death allow themselves to be banged and bullied and shouted at by children that hardly come up to their noses. So long as the boys keep with the herds they are safe, for not even the tiger will charge a mob of cattle. But if they straggle to pick flowers or hunt lizards, they are sometimes carried off. Mowgli went through the village street in the dawn, sitting on the back of Rama, the great herd bull; and the slaty-blue buffaloes, with their long, backward-sweeping horns and savage eyes, rose out of their byres, one by one, and followed him, and Mowgli made it very clear to the children with him that he was the master. He beat the buffaloes with a long, polished bamboo, and told Kamya, one of the boys, to graze the cattle by themselves, while he went on with the buffaloes, and to be very careful not to stray away from the herd.

An Indian grazing-ground is all rocks and scrub and tussocks and little ravines, among which the herds scatter and disappear. The buffaloes generally keep to the pools and muddy places, where they lie wallowing or basking in the warm mud for hours. Mowgli drove them on to the edge of the plain where the Waingunga River came out of the Jungle; then he dropped from Rama's neck, trotted off to a bamboo clump, and found Grey Brother. "Ah!" said Grey Brother. "I have waited here very many days. What is the meaning of this cattle-herding work?"

"It is an order," said Mowgli. "I am a village herd for a while. What news of Shere Khan?"

"He has come back to this country, and has waited here a long time for thee. Now he has gone off again, for the game is scarce. But he means to kill thee."

"Very good," said Mowgli. "So long as he is away do thou or one of the four brothers sit on that rock, so that I can see thee as I come out of the village. When he comes back wait for me in the ravine by the *dhâk*-tree in the centre of the plain. We need not walk into Shere Khan's mouth."

Then Mowgli picked out a shady place, and lay down and slept while the buffaloes grazed round him. Herding in India is one of the laziest things in the world. The cattle move and crunch, and lie down, and move on again, and they do not even low. They only grunt, and the buffaloes very seldom say anything, but get down into the muddy pools one after another, and work their way into the mud till only their noses and staring china-blue eyes show above the surface, and there they lie like logs. The sun makes the rocks dance in the heat, and the herd-children hear one kite (never any more) whistling almost out of sight overhead, and they know that if they died, or a cow died, that kite would sweep down, and the next kite miles away would see him drop and would follow, and the next, and the next, and almost before they were dead there would be a score of hungry kites come out of nowhere. Then they sleep and wake and sleep again, and weave little baskets of dried grass and put grasshoppers in them; or catch two praying-mantis and make them fight; or string a necklace of red and black Jungle nuts; or watch a lizard basking on a rock, or a snake hunting a frog near the wallows. Then they sing long, long songs with odd native quavers at the end of them, and the day seems longer than most people's whole lives, and perhaps they make a mud castle with mud figures of men and horses and buffaloes, and put reeds into the men's hands, and pretend that they are kings and the figures are their armies, or that they are gods to be worshipped. Then evening comes, and the children call, and the buffaloes lumber up out of the sticky mud with noises like gun-shots going off one after the other, and they all string across the grey plain back to the twinkling village lights.

Day after day Mowgli would lead the buffaloes out to their wallows, and day after day he would see Grey Brother's back a mile and a half away across the plain (so he knew that Shere Khan had not come back), and day after day he would lie on the grass listening to the noises round him, and dreaming of old days in the Jungle. If Shere Khan had made a false step with his lame paw up in the Jungles by the Waingunga, Mowgli would have heard him in those long, still mornings.

At last a day came when he did not see Grey Brother at the signal-place, and he laughed and headed the buffaloes for the ravine by the *dhâk*-tree, which was all covered with golden-red flowers. There sat Grey Brother, every bristle on his back lifted.

"He has hidden for a month to throw thee off thy guard. He crossed the ranges last night with Tabaqui, hotfoot on thy trail," said the wolf, panting.

Mowgli frowned. "I am not afraid of Shere Khan, but Tabaqui is very cunning."

"Have no fear," said Grey Brother, licking his lips a little. "I met Tabaqui in the dawn. Now he is telling all his wisdom to the kites, but he told *me* everything before I broke his back. Shere Khan's plan is to wait for thee at the village gate this evening – for thee and for no one else. He is lying up now in the big dry ravine of the Waingunga."

"Has he eaten today, or does he hunt empty?" said Mowgli, for the answer meant life or death to him.

"He killed at dawn – a pig – and he has drunk too. Remember, Shere Khan could never fast, even for the sake of revenge."

"Oh! Fool, fool! What a cub's cub it is! Eaten and drunk too, and he thinks that I shall wait till he has slept! Now, where does he lie up? If there were but ten of us we might pull him down as he lies. These buffaloes will not charge unless they wind him, and I cannot speak their language. Can we get behind his track so that they may smell it?"

"He swam far down the Waingunga to cut that off," said Grey Brother.

"Tabaqui told him that, I know. He would never have thought of it alone." Mowgli stood with his finger in his mouth, thinking. "The big ravine of the Waingunga. That opens out on the plain not half a mile from here. I can take the herd round through the Jungle to the head of the ravine and then sweep down – but he would slink out at the foot. We must block that end. Grey Brother, canst thou cut the herd in two for me?"

"Not I, perhaps – but I have brought a wise helper." Grey Brother trotted off and dropped into a hole. Then there lifted up a huge grey head that Mowgli knew well, and the hot air was filled with the most desolate cry of all the Jungle – the hunting-howl of a wolf at midday.

"Akela! Akela!" said Mowgli, clapping his hands. "I might have known that thou wouldst not forget me. We have a big work in hand. Cut the herd in two, Akela. Keep the cows and calves together, and the bulls and the plough-buffaloes by themselves."

The two wolves ran, ladies'-chain fashion, in and out of the herd, which snorted and threw up its head, and separated into two clumps. In one the cow-buffaloes stood, with their calves in the centre, and glared and pawed, ready, if a wolf would only stay still,

130

to charge down and trample the life out of him. In the other the bulls and the young bulls snorted and stamped; but, though they looked more imposing, they were much less dangerous, for they had no calves to protect. No six men could have divided the herd so neatly.

"What orders?" panted Akela. "They are trying to join again."

Mowgli slipped on to Rama's back. "Drive the bulls away to the left, Akela. Grey Brother, when we are gone, hold the cows together, and drive them into the foot of the ravine."

"How far?" said Grey Brother, panting and snapping.

"Till the sides are higher than Shere Khan can jump," shouted Mowgli. "Keep them there till we come down." The bulls swept off as Akela bayed, and Grey Brother stopped in front of the cows. They charged down on him and he ran just before them to the foot of the ravine, as Akela drove the bulls far to the left.

"Well done! Another charge and they are fairly started. Careful, now – careful, Akela. A snap too much, and the bulls will charge. *Huyah*! This is wilder work than driving black-buck. Didst thou think these creatures could move so swiftly?" Mowgli called.

"I have – have hunted these too in my time," gasped Akela in the dust. "Shall I turn them into the Jungle?"

"Ay, turn! Swiftly turn them! Rama is mad with rage. Oh, if I could only tell him what I need of him today!"

The bulls were turned to the right this time, and crashed into the standing thicket. The other herd-children, watching with the cattle half a mile away, hurried to the village as fast as their legs could carry them, crying that the buffaloes had gone mad and run away.

But Mowgli's plan was simple enough. All he wanted to do was to make a big circle uphill and get at the head of the ravine, and then take the bulls down it and catch Shere Khan between the bulls and the cows; for he knew that after a meal and a full drink Shere Khan would not be in any condition to fight or to clamber up the sides of the ravine. He was soothing the buffaloes now by voice, and Akela had dropped far to the rear, only whimpering once or twice to hurry the rear-guard. It was a long, long circle, for they did not wish to get too near the ravine and give Shere Khan warning. At last Mowgli rounded up the bewildered herd at the head of the ravine on a grassy patch that sloped down to the ravine itself. From that height you could see across the tops of the trees down to the plain below; but what Mowgli looked at was the sides of the ravine, and he saw with a great deal of satisfaction that they ran nearly straight up and down, while the vines and creepers that hung over them would give no foothold to a tiger who wanted to get on.

"Let them breathe, Akela," he said, holding up his hand. "They have not winded him yet. Let them breathe. I must tell Shere Khan who comes. We have him in the trap."

He put his hands to his mouth and shouted down the ravine – it was almost like shouting down a tunnel – and the echoes jumped from rock to rock.

After a long time there came back the drawling,

sleepy snarl of a full-fed tiger just wakened.

"Who calls?" said Shere Khan, and a splendid peacock fluttered up out of the ravine screeching.

"I, Mowgli. Cattle thief, it is time to come to the Council Rock! Down – hurry them down, Akela! Down, Rama, down!"

The herd paused for an instant at the edge of the slope, but Akela gave tongue in the full hunting-yell, and they pitched over one after the other, just as steamers shoot rapids, the sand and stones spurting up round them. Once started, there was no chance of stopping, and before they were fairly in the bed of the ravine Rama winded Shere Khan and bellowed.

"Ha! Ha!" said Mowgli, on his back. "Now thou knowest!" and the torrent of black horns, foaming muzzles, and staring eyes whirled down the ravine like boulders in flood-time; the weaker buffaloes being shouldered out to the sides of the ravine, where they tore through the creepers. They knew what the business was before them – the terrible charge of the buffalo-herd, against which no tiger can hope to stand. Shere Khan heard the thunder of their hoofs, picked himself up, and lumbered down the ravine, looking from side to side for some way of escape; but the walls of the ravine were straight, and he had to keep on, heavy with his dinner and his drink, willing to do anything rather than fight. The herd splashed through the pool he had just left, bellowing till the narrow cut rang. Mowgli heard an answering bellow from the foot of the ravine, saw Shere Khan turn (the tiger knew if the worst came to the worst it was better to meet the bulls than the cows with their calves), and then Rama tripped, stumbled, and went on again over something soft, and, with the bulls at his heels, crashed full into the other herd, while the weaker buffaloes were lifted clean off their feet by the shock of the meeting. That charge carried both herds out into the plain, goring and stamping and snorting. Mowgli watched his time, and slipped off Rama's neck, laying about him right and left with his stick.

"Quick, Akela! Break them up. Scatter them, or they will be fighting one another. Drive them away, Akela. *Hai*, Rama! *Hai*! *hai*! *hai*! my children. Softly now, softly! It is all over."

Akela and Grey Brother ran to and fro nipping the buffaloes' legs, and though the herd wheeled once to charge up the ravine again, Mowgli managed to turn Rama, and the others followed him to the wallows.

Shere Khan needed no more trampling. He was dead, and the kites were coming for him already.

"Brothers, that was a dog's death," said Mowgli, feeling for the knife he always carried in a sheath round his neck now that he lived with men. "But he would never have shown fight. His hide will look well on the Council Rock. We must get to work swiftly."

A boy trained among men would never have dreamed of skinning a ten-foot tiger alone, but Mowgli knew better than any one else how an animal's skin is fitted on, and how it can be taken off. But it was hard work, and Mowgli slashed and tore and grunted for an hour, while the wolves lolled out their tongues, or came forward and tugged as he ordered them.

Presently a hand fell on his shoulder, and looking up he saw Buldeo with the Tower musket. The children had told the village about the buffalo stampede, and Buldeo went out angrily, only too anxious to correct Mowgli for not taking better care of the herd. The wolves dropped out of sight as soon as they saw the man coming.

"What is this folly?" said Buldeo angrily. "To think that thou canst skin a tiger! Where did the buffaloes kill him? It is the Lame Tiger, too, and there is a hundred rupees on his head. Well, well, we will overlook thy letting the herd run off, and perhaps I will give thee one of the rupees of the reward when I have taken the skin to Khanhiwara." He fumbled in his waist-cloth for flint and steel, and stooped down to singe Shere Khan's whiskers. Most native hunters singe a tiger's whiskers to prevent his ghost haunting them.

"Hum!" said Mowgli, half to himself as he ripped

back the skin of a forepaw. "So thou wilt take the hide to Khanhiwara for the reward, and perhaps give me one rupee? Now it is in my mind that I need the skin for my own use. Heh! old man, take away that fire!"

"What talk is this to the chief hunter of the village? Thy luck and the stupidity of thy buffaloes have helped thee to this kill. The tiger has just fed, or he would have gone twenty miles by this time. Thou canst not even skin him properly, little beggar-brat, and forsooth I, Buldeo, must be told not to singe his whiskers. Mowgli, I will not give thee one anna of the reward, but only a very big beating. Leave the carcass!"

"By the Bull that bought me," said Mowgli, who was trying to get at the shoulder, "must I stay babbling to an old ape all noon? Here, Akela, this man plagues me."

Buldeo, who was still stooping over Shere Khan's head, found himself sprawling on the grass, with a grey wolf standing over him, while Mowgli went on skinning as though he were alone in all India.

"Ye-es," he said, between his teeth. "Thou art altogether right, Buldeo. Thou wilt never give me one anna of the reward. There is an old war between this lame tiger and myself – a very old war, and – I have won."

To do Buldeo justice, if he had been ten years younger he would have taken his chance with Akela had he met the wolf in the woods; but a wolf who obeyed the orders of this boy who had private wars with man-eating tigers was not a common animal. It was sorcery, magic of the worst kind, thought Buldeo, and he wondered whether the amulet round his neck would protect him. He lay as still as still, expecting every minute to see Mowgli turn into a tiger, too.

"Maharaj! Great King!" he said at last, in a husky whisper.

"Yes," said Mowgli, without turning his head, chuckling a little.

"I am an old man. I did not know that thou wast anything more than a herd-boy. May I rise up and go away, or will thy servant tear me to pieces?"

"Go, and peace go with thee. Only, another time do not meddle with my game. Let him go, Akela."

Buldeo hobbled away to the village as fast as he could, looking back over his shoulder in case Mowgli should change into something terrible. When he got to the village he told a tale of magic and enchantment and sorcery that made the priest look very grave.

Mowgli went on with his work, but it was nearly twilight before he and the wolves had drawn the great gay skin clear of the body.

"Now we must hide this and take the buffaloes home! Help me to herd them, Akela."

The herd rounded up in the misty twilight, and when they got near the village Mowgli saw lights, and heard the conches and bells blowing and banging. Half the village seemed to be waiting for him by the gate. "That is because I have killed Shere Khan," he said to himself; but a shower of stones whistled about his ears, and the villagers shouted: "Sorcerer! Wolf's brat! Jungle-demon! Go away! Get hence quickly, or the priest will turn thee into a wolf again. Shoot, Buldeo, shoot!"

The old Tower musket went off with a bang, and a

young buffalo bellowed in pain.

"More sorcery!" shouted the villagers. "He can turn bullets. Buldeo, that was *thy* buffalo."

"Now what is this?" said Mowgli, bewildered, as the stones flew thicker.

"They are not unlike the Pack, these brothers of thine," said Akela, sitting down composedly. "It is in my head that, if bullets mean anything, they would cast thee out."

"Wolf! Wolf's cub! Go away!" shouted the priest, waving a sprig of the sacred *tulsi* plant.

"Again? Last time it was because I was a man. This time it is because I am a wolf. Let us go, Akela."

A woman – it was Messua – ran across to the herd, and cried: "Oh, my son, my son! They say thou art a sorcerer who can turn himself into a beast at will. I do not believe, but go away or they will kill thee. Buldeo says thou art a wizard, but I know thou hast avenged Nathoo's death."

"Come back, Messua!" shouted the crowd. "Come back, or we will stone thee.

Mowgli laughed a little short ugly laugh, for a stone had hit him in the mouth. "Run back, Messua. This is one of the foolish tales they tell under the big tree at dusk. I have at least paid for thy son's life. Farewell; and run quickly, for I shall send the herd in more swiftly than their brickbats. I am no wizard, Messua. Farewell!"

"Now, once more, Akela," he cried. "Bring the herd in."

The buffaloes were anxious enough to get to the village. They hardly needed Akela's yell, but charged through the gate like a whirlwind, scattering the crowd right and left.

"Keep count!" shouted Mowgli scornfully. "It may be that I have stolen one of them. Keep count, for I will do your herding no more. Fare you well, children of men, and thank Messua that I do not come in with my wolves and hunt you up and down your street."

He turned on his heel and walked away with the Lone Wolf; and as he looked up at the stars he felt happy. "No more sleeping in traps for me, Akela. Let us get Shere Khan's skin and go away. No; we will not hurt the village, for Messua was kind to me."

When the moon rose over the plain, making it look all milky, the horrified villagers saw Mowgli, with two wolves at his heels and a bundle on his head, trotting across at the steady wolf's trot that eats up the long miles like fire. Then they banged the temple bells and blew the conches louder than ever; and Messua cried, and Buldeo embroidered the story of his adventures in the Jungle, till he ended by saying that Akela stood up on his hind legs and talked like a man.

The moon was just going down when Mowgli and the two wolves came to the hill of the Council Rock, and they stopped at Mother Wolf's cave.

"They have cast me out from the Man-Pack, Mother," shouted Mowgli, "but I come with the hide of Shere Khan to keep my word." Mother Wolf walked stiffly from the cave with the cubs behind her, and her eyes glowed as she saw the skin.

"I told him on that day, when he crammed his head and shoulders into this cave, hunting for thy life, Little Frog – I told him that the hunter would be the hunted. It is well done."

"Little Brother, it is well done," said a deep voice in the thicket. "We were lonely in the Jungle without thee," and Bagheera came running to Mowgli's bare feet. They clambered up the Council Rock together, and Mowgli spread the skin out on the flat stone where Akela used to sit, and pegged it down with four slivers of bamboo, and Akela lay down upon it, and called the old call to the Council, "Look – look well, O Wolves!" exactly as he had called when Mowgli was first brought there.

Ever since Akela had been deposed, the Pack had been without a leader, hunting and fighting at their own pleasure. But they answered the call from habit, and some of them were lame from the traps they had fallen into, and some limped from shot-wounds, and some were mangy from eating bad food, and many were missing; but they came to the Council Rock, all that were left of them, and saw Shere Khan's striped hide on the rock, and the huge claws dangling at the end of the empty, dangling feet. It was then that Mowgli made up a song without any rhymes, a song that came up into his throat all by itself, and he shouted it aloud, leaping up and down on the rattling skin, and beating time with his heels till he had no more breath left, while Grey Brother and Akela howled between the verses.

"Look well, O Wolves! Have I kept my word?" said Mowgli when he had finished; and the wolves bayed, "Yes," and one tattered wolf howled:

"Lead us again, O Akela. Lead us again, O Man-cub, for we be sick of this lawlessness, and we would be the Free People once more."

"Nay," purred Bagheera, "that may not be. When ye

are full-fed, the madness may come upon ye again. Not for nothing are ye called the Free People. Ye fought for freedom, and it is yours. Eat it, O Wolves."

"Man-Pack and Wolf-Pack have cast me out," said Mowgli. "Now I will hunt alone in the Jungle."

"And we will hunt with thee," said the four cubs.

So Mowgli went away and hunted with the four cubs in the Jungle from that day on. But he was not always alone, because years afterwards he became a man and married.

But that is a story for grown-ups.

Farthing Wood,
the Adventure Begins

by Colin Dann

As long as the otters live in Farthing Wood, they are protected from humans. But when the otters start stealing food from the other animals the foxes decide to take action. Lead by Lean Vixen and Stout Fox, they ignore Sage Hedgehog's warnings and drive the otters from the wood, where one by one they perish. Soon only Long-Whiskers is left. But in the wood disaster looms as disease spreads and the humans move in...

The grassland around Farthing Wood shrank steadily as the human construction site began to take shape. The Farthing Wood animals, for the most part, tried to ignore the fact. But some of them recalled the otters' boasts. They remembered how there had, in truth, been no human activity when the otters lived by the stream. And they remembered how the foxes and others had plotted to rid themselves of the clever animals, and, in particular, that the foxes had joined together to drive the otters out. Rabbits and hares had already lost their chosen homes in the grassy areas they loved best. Some of the more thoughtful animals wondered now if that was only the start.

"Do you think that our set will always be here?" Young Badger asked his father one day.

"Of course it will," Kindly Badger replied at once. "Why, generation after generation of badgers have been born and raised here. It's… it's… *unthinkable* that that could ever change." He glanced at his mate for corroboration, as though perhaps needing reassurance himself.

"Don't worry," she said softly to the youngster. "You'll grow old here, of that I'm quite sure."

The young male couldn't think beyond that point and was happy.

The foxes didn't worry themselves about past events. The otters had gone and they thought that was a good thing. Yet Stout Fox would have been prepared to humble himself and ask an otter's advice about the sickness of his vixen if an otter had been around for him to do so.

Stout Vixen lay listlessly in their earth. She regretted her failure to be guided by her mate and to shun any voles as food. She hadn't cared for his over-protection. But he had been right. The sickness had taken hold of her and wouldn't go away. Each day she felt a little worse. She tried to eat what little Stout Fox brought her, so that at least she would have the strength to bring her cubs into the world when the time came. But gradually she came to realise that the cubs might be infected too, even if disease didn't claim her before they had a chance of life.

Stout Fox was beside himself with worry. There was no creature he could consult who had the secret of the cure. He watched the vixen wilt and sink a little more with every dawn. In desperation he set off through the Wood one evening in quest of Sage Hedgehog. As he went he told himself it was unlikely that the hedgehog could be of real assistance, but even if the old creature should offer one grain of comfort it would be worthwhile.

Sage Hedgehog was even more morose than the fox. The wasted opportunity of the Assembly had depressed him utterly. There was now, it seemed, no hope of alerting the stubborn and feckless Farthing Wood animals to their plight. Then, as he chewed monotonously on a long worm, thinking dire thoughts, Stout Fox appeared to interrupt his reverie.

"Old prophet hedgehog, I beg you to help," the fox blurted out. "If you know anything about the otters' methods in curing sickness, tell me."

Sage Hedgehog paused in his meal. "Your mate is worse?"

"Day by day."

"I am sorry for that. But I fear you are too late to save her. You've brought this misery on yourselves, for there is now no one who has the secret. The otters kept it to themselves."

Stout Fox sat on his haunches in despair. "Is there nothing I can do?" he asked.

"Do you know where the otters went after you foxes drove them from here?"

"No."

"They're probably widely scattered by this time. But

144

if you could find them – any of them – and persuade them to return, that would be your salvation." The old hedgehog suddenly perked up, as though there might just be a glimmer of hope. "Indeed," he resumed in a stronger voice, "you *must* find them. For the otters are the salvation of all of us and the Wood itself."

Stout Fox was encouraged. He looked more resolute. "You're right! Only they can halt the humans' progress. I realise that now. I'll go and search for them and, if I can, I'll take others to help in the search. I won't rest until I find them!" He turned and ran back towards his earth. He would need to find food enough for his vixen to last her until his return.

Stout Vixen received his news without enthusiasm. "It's useless," she muttered. "You'll never locate the otters. I shall be dead in a few days. Nothing can prevent that."

But the big fox wouldn't be put off. "I think you're wrong. And it would be contemptible not to try. I'll fetch food for you before I leave. Promise me you'll try to hold on."

"Very well," she whispered. "You have my word."

⁂

Once he had ensured that the vixen had managed to eat at least some of the titbits he had fetched for her, Stout Fox set off to recruit some helpers. He had no close associates and wondered where to begin. He decided that any swift-footed animal with the keen senses of a hunter would be useful in the search. Lightning Weasel dashed across his path.

"Stop!" the fox cried. "Wait!"

The weasel turned and looked at the larger animal

curiously. "Well? What is it?" Stout Fox trotted over.

"That's near enough, if you don't want me to run," Lightning Weasel said sharply. A fox was not a beast he wanted too close to him. "I don't believe the badger's Oath thing is still in force?"

Stout Fox blinked. "Oath? What oath?" His mind was on other things. Then he remembered. "Oh, that. I think not. I want to ask for your help."

"Help? From me?" the weasel queried in astonishment.

"Yes, I'm going to look for the otters. You see, I need their knowledge to save my mate."

"Oh, the sickness. Yes, we heard all about that at the Assembly. But this is a bit rich. You drove the otters away and now you want me to help you bring them back. That's your problem, I think."

"I know it sounds odd. I regret now what we foxes did. We all need them here. Without them what future is there for Farthing Wood?"

"Too late for regrets, I'm afraid. No, count me out. I've no time to waste on a fool's errand and, besides, you're no friend to me, so why should I help?"

"But surely, you know how I feel," Stout Fox said dejectedly. "Your own mate died of the sickness."

"That's right. And now I have another mate. If yours dies, you'll soon find another too. That's Nature, isn't it?" Lightning Weasel wasn't prepared to listen any further and bolted into the undergrowth.

Stout Fox sighed and continued on his errand. He began to realise that there wouldn't be much help forthcoming except from other foxes. He did approach Sly Stoat but there was no sympathy from that quarter either.

"*I* don't want the otters back. They took our food from our mouths. When we laid the trail of disease for them, I couldn't have foreseen how I would be repaid in kind. Now you're reaping the same reward. The otters have avenged themselves on us and there's no escaping it."

∞

Stout Fox accepted that he must look for assistance from his own kind. But he was no luckier with other foxes. These animals, the very ones who had combined to drive out the otter population, scoffed at the notion of inviting them back.

"You're mad," one said. "If we'd wanted them here in the first place, they'd still be around."

"Though *we* might not be," added another, "the way our food was being thieved."

"We're sorry for your mate," Lean Vixen told him. "She could have exercised more caution. But you really can't expect us to fight your battles for you."

"He's only asking for a little help in his search," Lean Fox reminded her, as usual the more sympathetic listener. "I could perhaps go with him for a while."

"And leave me to fend alone for our cubs?" the vixen retorted. "Don't even consider it!"

"No, no, she's right," Stout Fox murmured, bowing to the inevitable. "I shall go alone. I was wrong to try to involve others in my difficulties."

When he was out of earshot Lean Vixen growled, "And woe betide any otters he manages to round up. Because they'll find a funny sort of welcome awaiting them in Farthing Wood."

Long-Whiskers awoke at the end of the night. Rain was falling heavily and she felt cold. She heaved herself further under the hedgerow. Her coat was thoroughly damp but the raindrops helped to revive her. As dawn broke she became aware of the movements of birds. There were nests along that hedgerow and the parent birds, at first light, resumed their quest for food for the nestlings. Long-Whiskers watched them flying to and fro, and she was able to locate the various nests by the twittering of the hungry chicks, and also by the places where the adults entered and left the hedge. Despite her painful wounds, Long-Whiskers felt hungry. She began to raid those nests within reach, one by one. The young birds stood no chance. Their parents cried their distress as they saw the hunter in the hedgerow, knowing they were powerless to intervene.

In the daylight Long-Whiskers licked her chops as she rested again out of sight. She had a full stomach and already she felt stronger.

❦

Under cover of darkness Stout Fox paddled across the stream and skirted the remaining grassland. He knew the otters would have first crossed the grassland to escape the angry foxes' pursuit. The building works loomed ominously in the distance. All was quiet, but the fox smelt human smells and the unfamiliar odours of their machines and materials hanging on the air. Above all there was the stench of mud. He saw a rabbit skip across the fringe of the muddy area and then disappear underground. He was surprised by just how close the rabbits' burrows were to the human presence. The grassland had been inhabited by rabbits and hares for as long as any animal in Farthing Wood could remember. Now some of that area had been destroyed and they had had to move their homes into the Wood. Thus they were more vulnerable to marauding foxes, stoats and weasels.

Stout Fox steered clear of the parts changed by the humans. He discovered that this area extended farther than he and probably any other creature had realised. No animal, save the rabbits, had ventured anywhere near it. He thought it his duty to describe to those who would listen what he had seen.

"But that must come later," he told himself. "First I have to sniff out the hiding-place of those clever otters."

∽

The hares and most of the rabbits had indeed migrated into Farthing Wood itself. But, in addition to the added danger of their being within easier reach of their habitual predators, there was pressure for space. A single warren remained in use outside the Wood. It was one of the rabbits from here that Stout Fox had noticed. There were many young – some still suckling – living in the network of tunnels. The rabbits, though fearful of the human din, had almost grown used to the noise and alarms created every day by the builders and their machines. By day they cowered quietly in their burrows. None went above ground until each last sound made by the humans had died away. And even then they waited and waited, finally peeping out to see if it was safe to browse. Usually one of them gave the all-clear signal and then the adults and adolescents would gladly run free and begin to feed.

A period of rain followed Stout Fox's departure. The area around the warren became increasingly muddy. The burrow entrances and the tunnels seeped with mud and the rabbits were very miserable. They wished they had been able to move home. But the babies couldn't yet be moved.

The rain didn't, of course, prevent the humans from proceeding with their affairs. And, to the unfortunate rabbits, it seemed as though the noise and bustle was coming perilously close. They squatted in their slimy tunnels and passages, ears pricked and noses permanently a-quiver. Outside a bulldozer roared and slithered, teetering on one side, then the other, as its angle was dictated by the unstable mud. All at once daylight flooded into the warren. The bulldozer had carved out a huge mass of soil, ripping into one edge of the warren itself. The rabbits fled into the deeper heart of the system. But they were not safe. The bulldozer, having dumped its latest load, reversed and trundled forward again like a juggernaut. Nothing could divert it. Its course was set. The warren was in its path.

As if opening its jaws for another mighty bite, the machine ploughed into the centre of the warren, tearing up the entire labyrinth of runs, nesting burrows with its nursing mothers, babies, and most of the other fugitive rabbits. The load was hoisted high. Rabbits leapt or fell to the ground in terror. Others dangled from the mud, half in and half out of a mangled run. The bulldozer swung round, tipping more animals out as it turned, then depositing the remainder in a pile of soil and sludge where they squirmed like so many worms. They were trapped by the impacted mud and

150

couldn't wriggle clear.

By this time cries from other workers on the site had alerted the earth-mover's driver to what had happened. He quickly turned off his engine as he saw the rabbits struggling and thrashing in the morass, while others twitched helplessly on the ground where they had been flung or had fallen. Only a few animals managed to escape unharmed. A look of consternation passed across the face of the driver who had quite unwittingly caused the destruction of the warren. He jumped from his cab. Other men squelched through the mud to try to free the half-buried animals. When they found the babies, some still beneath their mothers' bodies, they called out to each other in mutual pity and compassion. The driver looked particularly upset. The men did what they could for the animals who had survived, clumsily trying to clean them up and then setting them free. The few rabbits who were unhurt bounded into the Wood.

There was now a kind of bank of mud and grass remaining where the greedy jaws of the earth-mover hadn't yet reached. Inside this bank the last remnants of the rabbits from the warren hid in the few vestiges of holes and passages the machine had missed. They waited, passive victims, for the monster to gobble them up. They were exposed; cut off from any further retreat. There was nowhere to run. Yet somehow they seemed to be forgotten. They didn't hear the roar of the machine that they expected to hear. And they were left, to their amazement, undisturbed. The humans, strangely affected by what had recently happened, left that part of the site alone for the rest of the day and began working elsewhere.

Rain continued to fall. The treacherous mud absorbed more and more water until it was saturated. Puddles formed on its surface. The bank, too, was saturated through and gouts of mud broke away from it and slid down its side. The ground there was very unstable. Cold, wet and frightened, the rabbits inside the bank shivered through the day in a huddle. When darkness brought a cessation of human activity, one danger was replaced by another. The exposed holes in the bank were an open invitation to any hunter who picked up the rabbits' scent.

∽

The foxes, of course, did so. There were more rabbits in the Wood, trying to enter other families' burrows and dens after fleeing the humans. Some were accepted, but in other places there was overcrowding already. The foxes went on a killing spree. Stoats and weasels joined in. A number of rabbits, driven from one side to the other in their efforts to escape, even began to run back to the muddy building site which had recently been their home. A few predators pursued them. Amongst these were Lean Fox and Lean Vixen.

"The cubs must do without their mother for a while," the vixen had told her mate. "I shall eat rabbit tonight, and I don't mean to be left out of the chase."

Lean Fox knew better than to gainsay her. The two ran together. They startled an adult rabbit on the fringe of the Wood and raced in pursuit. Another rabbit ran from their approach. Lean Fox chose this one, the vixen the other. It was soon apparent that these rabbits had no bolt-holes. They dashed out of the Wood and on to the top of the bank.

"Catch it, catch it," Lean Vixen called to her mate as she hurtled after her own quarry.

The rabbits hesitated. The foxes' hot breath ruffled their fur. They leapt and landed in the sticky morass of mud where so many of their own kind had already met their fate. Lean Fox had no time to draw back. He crashed after them, the weight of his body embedding him in the ooze. He saw Lean Vixen falter on the brink.

"Don't jump!" he cried. "It's a trap!"

Lean Vixen watched her mate thrashing about in his attempts to free himself from the quagmire. She saw the rabbits – their prey – beginning to pull their lighter bodies out of the mud. The rain beat down on them all mercilessly.

"They're getting away!" Lean Vixen shrilled, her one concern above all else being the loss of her prize. Lean Fox struggled harder, but the cloying mud seemed to engulf his body. Lean Vixen teetered indecisively. Suddenly beneath her feet she spied another rabbit trembling in its inadequate hole. Instinctively she began to dig, more and more furiously as the urge to kill enveloped her. The hole gaped and crumbled and, as she lunged, the entire bank collapsed, burying her mate and the fleeing rabbits, while she was brought crashing down with it. Where the bank broke, a rush of water from the swollen stream flooded through the breach, and Lean Vixen was swamped by more mud, carried by the spate. The water poured over her head and the few rabbits who had been sheltering in the unstable bank were drowned with her. Some small trees, whose roots were ripped out of the soil by the subsidence, fell on their sides. The breach, blocked by tree-trunks, vegetation and gathering silt, was sealed. But a new muddy pond had formed on the edge of the building site. On its surface two dead foxes and a number of rabbits floated: a testimony to the human menace. The first animals had been killed, the first trees had been felled. Moreover a small, but ominous, gap had appeared like an open wound in Farthing Wood.

Beyond this place of drama Long-Whiskers was ready to continue her return journey. It was dark. The rain beat against the hedgerow with a relentless rhythm. She shook her coat vigorously and set off. Recognisable features that she passed on her way cheered her and strengthened her determination. Traffic noise reminded her of the road she must cross eventually. "It won't be so formidable now I'm alone," she said to herself, thinking of Lame Otter's vulnerability. But at once her thoughts were full of her own solitariness and she felt forlorn.

"You are my companions," she whispered to her unborn cubs. "Though I travel alone, we travel together."

She stopped just short of the road, hiding in a leafy garden. Her sores were healing and she was almost able to put them out of her mind.

※

From the opposite direction Stout Fox set his face against the lash of the rain. The taint of otter tracks was still strong enough for his sensitive nose to detect. He was pleased with his progress. His ailing vixen was constantly on his mind. He knew time was not on her side. He pictured her, head on paws, lying morosely in their den.

"I must save her. I *will* save her." Stout Fox kept up this chant as he went, urging himself on to a greater effort and pace. "The otters have the secret, and I have their scent."

☙

In the morning Nervous Squirrel saw the devastation. "A hole! A hole in Farthing Wood!"

And Jay screamed, "Dead foxes! Dead rabbits! Who's next? Who's next?"

☙

The deaths of Lean Fox and Lean Vixen, as well as the way Farthing Wood had been penetrated, soon became common knowledge. While the humans busied themselves with cleaning up operations, news of their advance, slight though it was, spread through the Wood like a flame.

"I told you, I warned you," Sage Hedgehog cried bitterly to anyone who would listen. And now most did. "They intend to destroy us. Little by little, Farthing Wood will fall. We're in their grasp and they won't let go. Only the otters held the key to our preservation. And where are they now?"

"Stout Fox is searching for them," Sly Stoat said. "Oh, how I regret I didn't go with him!"

"It's never too late," Kindly Badger said. "He needs help. He asked for it and was rejected. And the Wood is at the mercy of the humans if he fails. We have a duty to go. We can't depend on one creature alone for our salvation."

"Were I young I'd be with the fox now," Sage Hedgehog said sadly. "But, as I'm constantly reminded,

I'm old and forgetful of the ways of the young."

"You have more than played your part already," Kindly Badger assured him. "If we had listened more to you at the beginning, things might have been very different." He turned to Sly Stoat. "There's no time left for talking. We should bring all the animals together who want to help save Farthing Wood, and leave this very night. If the otters are still around, one of us should be able to discover them."

There was quite a gathering that crept carefully from the Wood in the dead of night and dispersed beyond the humans' workings in the all-important search. Stout Vixen had tottered to the earth entrance to watch the departure. It was impossible for her not to know what was afoot. Murmurs, rumours and chatter had been audible above ground for hours. She wondered how far her mate had travelled and whether he had met with any success. She was battling to fight off the sinister clutches of the disease – forcing herself to eat, lapping at raindrops, and determined to 'hold on' for Stout Fox's return as she had promised him.

❦

Long-Whiskers awoke in the garden. A loud clatter outside the house disturbed her. At once she tensed, her muscles taut and ready to power her into flight. There was nothing to be seen, but she sensed a presence. Whatever it was, it wasn't human and she relaxed a fraction. A feeling of weariness overcame her. She had over-exerted herself the previous night and was reminded now of her weak state. She must lie low and conserve her strength for a while. She thought of her abandoned holt. How long ago it seemed when she and the other otters had played so freely and carelessly in the snow! And how ill-deserved was their fate at the hands of the foxes. She thought of them with hatred. The misery she and others had suffered, the futility of their escape from Farthing Wood, the accidents, the deaths – all as a result of the foxes' jealousy and persecution.

Long-Whiskers lay down again amongst the drenched plants in the garden. She didn't feel ready to eat yet and wanted only to rest. Then all at once she saw the creature who had caused the clatter. It was a fox.

The fox was a well-built animal. It had smelt meat outside the house and had overturned a dustbin to get at it. It was making a meal from human left-overs. Long-Whiskers' heart beat fast. She recognised the animal at once as Stout Fox, the most powerful of the foxes from Farthing Wood. She shrank back, unsure whether to remain or run. What was the fox doing there? Why had it left the Wood? The conclusion she reached was one that made her shudder. It was hunting for her!

Naturally Long-Whiskers knew nothing of the change of heart regarding the otters in Farthing Wood. She remembered only the animosity and the savagery of the foxes. She believed now that Stout Fox had come to seek out every otter; to ensure that the last of them was killed so that there could never be any recurrence of the rivalry over food. And she suspected also that there were others of his kind around, bent on the same task. She was in terrible danger. She thought of her cubs. She must preserve their chance of survival at all costs. She knew all about the foxes' powerful senses of smell and hearing. She didn't think she could avoid discovery in the garden.

Slowly, painfully slowly, Long-Whiskers pulled herself from the vegetation and began to move off. A flicker of movement might have given her away, but the fox's head was turned towards the house. Long-Whiskers increased her speed. Now the rustle of her body made Stout Fox look round. He sniffed the air. He saw where the plants waved and parted. He ran forward. Long-Whiskers could think only of escape. She broke into a run and headed for the road. It was not late and there was traffic passing at intervals. With the fox behind her, the otter had to gamble. To be caught by the fox she believed would mean certain death. As for the human machines, there was just a possibility she could dodge them.

Stout Fox saw her intention. "Don't run from me!" he barked. "You don't understand: I haven't come to harm you. I've come for your help."

Long-Whiskers was oblivious to his cries. She was concentrating as hard as she could on choosing her moment. She saw that the swift machines had separate movements. There were spaces between their passing. But she had no idea of their speed. To an animal it was unimaginable.

"Stop!" the fox barked. He could see her desperation. "You'll be killed! The machines. They –" His last bark was muffled by the roar of a huge lorry. When it had passed Long-Whiskers had disappeared. She was neither on his side of the road, nor across on the other. He sniffed the air for her scent. It was there. He looked down the road. And then he saw her. One of the giant wheels of the lorry had struck Long-Whiskers a glancing blow, sending her spinning through the air. She had landed some metres away, farther up the road, and was trying to drag herself from its surface.

"She's injured," Stout Fox muttered. "Her legs are crushed. I must try to pull her free."

Traffic continued to pass. No vehicle stopped, but each one went around the struggling otter. Stout Fox trotted forward. Selfishly, he had no thought at that moment of the otter's vital importance to Farthing Wood. His one idea was to obtain the information he needed for his vixen's survival. As soon as it was safe, he crossed the road.

Long-Whiskers saw him approaching. She knew she had no defences. "So you've come to finish me off?" she gasped. The fox ignored her. He grasped her by the nape of the neck and lifted her in his jaws. She was heavy. He laid her in soft grass in the nearest field. She stared up at him with glassy eyes.

"The machine has done the job you came to do," she panted.

Stout Fox blinked uncomprehendingly. "Where are the others?" he asked.

Long-Whiskers sighed a long sigh. "There *are* no others. I'm the last. And in me die the last of the Farthing Wood otters."

"But you mustn't die. Not yet," Stout Fox pleaded. "You saved yourself from the sickness. Give me the knowledge, I beg you, to save my mate."

A realisation seemed to dawn in Long-Whiskers' eyes. "So that's why you came?" she whispered.

Much distressed, Stout Fox recalled his other

motivation. "No, not that alone. I came to find you and to bring you home. Our home. The home we all share."

"Ha! There'll be no home for me," Long-Whiskers answered him with bitterness. "And neither for my cubs."

"You have cubs?" Stout Fox exclaimed. "Then you're not the last."

"My cubs die with me."

The fox understood and, remembering all that had passed, a great sadness overcame him. He knew the foxes bore the blame for the present situation. "Forgive us for bringing you to this plight," he muttered brokenly.

Long-Whiskers didn't reply.

"I would like to help you if I can," the fox resumed.

"I'm beyond help."

"Perhaps not. Farthing Wood is close. We need you."

"Oh yes," the otter gasped with the irony. "For giving you my knowledge. Ha! When we lived together, foxes and otters, you didn't want our knowledge. Only our extinction."

This was horribly true and Stout Fox had no reply to give.

"Why should I, then, help *you*?" Long-Whiskers demanded.

"I have no right to ask."

"Your mate is sick? What kind of sickness?"

Stout Fox explained.

Long-Whiskers was silent for a long while. Then she murmured, "There is no help I can give you, even if I would. I was not one of the otters who fell sick from disease. It's true some of us who were sick were able to heal ourselves. I don't know how."

"You – you have no idea?" Stout Fox asked hopelessly.

"Perhaps a plant... I can't say..." The otter's head drooped. She seemed about to expire.

"Please, what can I do for you?" the fox beseeched her earnestly.

Several moments passed. The otter rallied. "As we're... no longer enemies," she said weakly, "maybe you could stay with me until..." She left the rest unsaid; it wasn't necessary to finish.

Stout Fox was in a dilemma. He greatly wished to make recompense for the tragedy he had brought about. On the other hand time was running out for his vixen and he was desperate to get back to her. The otter bitch looked as if she couldn't last much longer. He tried to be patient. "I'll wait with you," he said softly.

❧

Some of the other animals who were searching – the swiftest runners – had covered a lot of ground in very little time. Lightning Weasel was the fastest of these. He detected the musky odour of fox. He looked around. He saw Stout Fox lying, nose to tail, a little way ahead. Was he asleep? The weasel crept forward. He saw that there was another animal by the fox's side.

Stout Fox opened one eye. "You have nothing to fear from me," he said. "I'm not hunting, although *you* clearly are. Why have you come so far?"

"To look for the otters," Lightning Weasel squeaked.

Stout Fox's ears pricked. "Then your search is at an

end," he said.

The weasel began to understand. "You – you have found one?"

"Come nearer."

Lightning Weasel trotted up. "Is the otter dead?"

"Not quite. And why are you searching now? You didn't want to come with me when I asked you."

The weasel explained about the hole in Farthing Wood, the dead foxes and the rabbits.

Stout Fox sat bolt upright. "Which foxes were killed?" he demanded.

The weasel told him. Stout Fox sank back. "Well, you and the other beasts and myself, too – we're all too late. The otters have been wiped out. I tried to save this one here, but failed. She told me she's the last. When she dies perhaps Farthing Wood will begin to die too."

Lightning Weasel sniffed at Long-Whiskers. She was quite still and, seeing this, the weasel for once became still too. He and Stout Fox waited together quietly and, later, other animals found their way to the spot. Sly Stoat and Kindly Badger were among them. Together they waited in silence as though doing penance for the demise of the Farthing Wood otters.

Before dawn all the animals were on their way home. Subdued and down-hearted, they drifted back in ones and twos to their dens and burrows. The significance of Long-Whiskers' death weighed heavily on all of them.

As light began to fill the sky, Stout Fox headed for the stream in a last effort to unlock the secret of the otters' knowledge. He felt that somewhere along the water's edge where they had chosen their holts, there might be a clue waiting to be discovered. He cast his eyes along the bank and around the territory. Then he swam the stream and did the same on the side bordering the Wood. He stared at each plant, trying to assess its value and hoping for enlightenment. Nothing struck him as being unusual.

"Oh, those otters," he moaned to himself. "Even now they're dead and gone they still haunt me. How was it they were able to do things we other animals can't? What made them so different?" He ran along the bank, shaking his head. All at once an idea came into his mind. "There was one thing that made them different from us," he murmured. "Their love of water, their wonderful skill in diving and swimming. Perhaps there's something in the water that's beneficial..." He bent and lapped experimentally, but there was nothing to taste then, any more than the hundreds of other times he had drunk from it.

"I hate to return to the vixen with no hope," he muttered. "But I mustn't leave her any longer. I've tried to find the cure. I've done all I can."

He ran on into the Wood, eager to see Stout Vixen again, yet dreading to find her worse than before. He came upon her asleep in their earth. He was loath to wake her, but she sensed his company.

"You're back then," she whispered. "I – I managed to hold on."

"You look so weak..."

"Did you learn anything?" she asked with a glimmer of hope.

Stout Fox looked down. "The otters are all dead. Their secret died with them."

The vixen heaved a long sigh as if finally she was letting go. But Stout Fox said quickly, "Listen. Can you walk? I want you to come to the stream. Try to drink some water. It may do some good."

"What's the point?" she asked him hoarsely. "I might as well die here as there."

"There's just a chance. Please – for me and our cubs."

"Our cubs will never be born."

"You mustn't say that! You *must* try."

Wearily, painfully, the vixen got to her feet. Stout Fox nuzzled her and nudged her to the entrance hole. She swayed, unused to any kind of exertion. Patiently and with sympathy he encouraged her to walk. For the vixen, it seemed each step was more difficult than the last.

The edge of the Wood was a long way off. They paused often to allow her to rest. The noise of machinery echoed through the woodland, emphasising the peril that each creature now recognised was its inheritance. Even Jay's screeches of alarm were drowned by the brutality of the bulldozers. Stout Fox had no need to explain the state of affairs to his mate. She knew enough to realise that, if ever their cubs were born, they would be born into a hostile world.

Somehow Stout Vixen got herself to the fringes of Farthing Wood. By then it was growing dark again. She gasped, "Where is the nearest water? My legs won't take me any further."

"Here. Just over here," the fox called. The rain at last had ceased and the pale moon was reflected in the dark swollen stream.

The vixen crawled on her belly to the bank and let her muzzle drop into the water.

"There's a lot of growth there." Stout Fox pointed out a mass of cressy plants tangled underwater. "Come to where I'm standing. The stream runs clearer here."

Stout Vixen raised her head. Strands of the plants were draped over her muzzle. "Growth or no growth," she panted, "this is where I stop." She bent and drank greedily. The water was cold and, while drinking it, she swallowed some cress. She sucked in a good mouthful of the plant and chewed it, relishing its clean peppery taste. Then she lay her head on her paws and fell asleep where she was.

Later the vixen awoke and noticed at once that the dull ache in the pit of her stomach which had troubled her for so long had disappeared. She felt less listless than she had done for many days. She looked up. Stout Fox was absent. She scrambled to her feet, still weak but tremendously hungry. As she savoured her new feeling of well-being her mate came trotting from the Wood. A dead rabbit dangled from his jaws. He had scarcely dropped it before Stout Vixen seized it ravenously and began to tear off mouthfuls.

"Well, this is a transformation," the fox commented delightedly. "The water, then, has been of some help."

"I think it was the plant," Stout Vixen mumbled, her mouth full. "It's purged me."

"The plant?" Stout Fox whispered, recalling Long-Whiskers' words. "So that's it! Yes," he cried, "of course. That's how the otters were healed. Water-plants!" He peered into the stream. "Will you take some more?" he asked eagerly.

"Certainly," the vixen replied. "I intend to make a full recovery. I shall need to build up my strength again quickly."

"The cubs!"

"Yes. You have been a good mate. You made me struggle here almost against my will. The stream did hold the clue and you were right to insist."

Stout Fox was jubilant. He had saved his vixen and, in that joyful knowledge, the fate of Farthing Wood was for a while forgotten.

∞

Two days later Stout Vixen gave birth to four cubs. The poison that had infected her caused three of them to be still-born. The fourth, a male cub, by way of compensation looked to be robust. Stout Vixen removed the rest of her litter from the earth with resignation.

"One little cub to face an uncertain future," Stout Fox murmured sadly.

"But a future with some hope if he has your wits," Stout Vixen remarked.

The Crowstarver

by Dick King-Smith

Spider was discovered as a baby in a lambing pen and grew up instinctively relating to animals. From sheep and cows, to otters and foxes, Spider loves them all and can imitate any of their noises. Then Percy Pound the farmer offers him a job making a very different noise – to scare the crows away from his crops...

The following Monday was to be Spider's first day at work. It was quite a cold morning, and Kathie had sent him off properly dressed against the weather. He wore an old army greatcoat that had belonged to Tom in his brief days of soldiering and was a good deal too big and long for his son. It reached down to Spider's ankles, and the waist had to be drawn in by a length of binder twine. In one pocket of this coat was a packet containing bread and cheese and in the other a bottle of cold tea.

He left the cottage in company with his father, and they parted at the bottom of the drove, Tom to go on up it to the shepherd's hut, Spider under orders to go down the road to the farmyard and report to

Percy Pound.

"You just do as you're told, Spider lad," said Tom, "and you won't come to no harm."

Spider grinned and set off in his usual bent-forward flat-footed way, but though his feet turned outwards as ever, his arms, which normally hung by his sides, now swung vigorously in what he obviously considered a soldierly manner.

Ephraim Stanhope the horseman was always earliest in the stables, so that Percy Pound's first words on arrival were, as usual.

"Morning, Eph."

"Morning, Percy."

"Dunno if I told you," said Percy, "but Tom Sparrow's boy's starting today. I'm going to take him up to Maggs' Corner, to keep the birds off. We drilled it with wheat last week."

"Oh is that what he's on about?" said Ephraim. "'What you doing here?' I said to him, and he says 'Croaks! Bad croaks!' and flaps his arms about."

"Oh, he's here already, is he?"

"Ar, and I'll tell you something for nothing, Percy, he's either fearless or foolish. He's been round all the horses already, talking to 'em, if you can call it talking, mumbling more like, and gentling them, and they've all stood there like lambs."

"Never!" said Percy.

"Some of them's quiet enough as you know," said Ephraim, "but old Flower, she don't like kids anywhere near her as a rule, and Em'ly, she do lash out at strangers, and as for that Pony, he do bite – took a nip out of our Albie just afore he went off to the Yeomanry.

But this Spider, he ain't afeared of any of them and they seem to know it."

Before Percy had time to comment on all this, the rest of the farm men came into the stables, first Red and Rhode Ogle and then the three Butts. Frank and Phil were biggish men, and between them their uncle looked even smaller than usual. Billy was approaching sixty-five now but he could still do a good day's work, and, had there been a donkey on Outoverdown Farm, he would without doubt have talked the hind leg off it.

"Yur, 'tis brass monkey weather," he piped now, rubbing his hands together, and to the foreman who stood leaning his left arm on Flower's rump as usual, he said, "I 'opes you got a nice warm job for me today, Percy. I ain't so young as I was."

"Go on, Billy," said Rhode Ogle. "You don't look a day over ninety."

"Shut thy trap, young Rhode!" squeaked Billy angrily. "Eighteen hundred and seventy-four I were born and that's a bleddy long time ago, I can tell ee. You wait till you gets to my age, which I don't never suppose you will, feather-brained young idjut, got no more sense than one of your dad's cockerels, and they don't wear no bleddy glasses what's more, chances are you'll fall off the top of a hay mow and break your bleddy neck afore you'm much older and don't think old Billy'll come to your bleddy funeral neither."

Percy opened his mouth to say 'That's enough' but before he could speak, Billy suddenly fell silent, for Spider had come down Flower's off side from where he had been standing at her head, hidden from the men. Seeing Percy's attitude, he copied it. The mare turned her head at the touch of Spider's right arm on her rump, but then turned back, unconcerned, and pulled a wisp of hay from her crib. The Butts and the Ogles gawped at this sight. They all knew that the shire mare, though generally tractable, had no liking for children and would shift about and stamp her great feet if one came near. Yet here she was, placid as an old sheep beside this odd-looking boy in the long greatcoat. Even Billy lost his tongue.

"Right," said Percy Pound sharply (the east wind was making his knee hurt). "Perhaps now you'll let me get a word in edgewise, Billy. But first of all, this is Tom and Kathie's boy as you all know, and he's starting work today, going to do a bit of crowstarving. Now, he's got his little problems, Spider has, and I don't want anyone poking fun at him just because he don't speak too well. Now then, Spider, you tell 'em what you're going to do today."

Spider looked around at the men confronting him and saw that each wore some sort of a smile, and he grinned back and said "Spider scare croaks!"

"Good boy," said Percy. "Now you just wait awhile, and then I'll take you up to Maggs' Corner and start you off."

When he had given out his instructions to the other men and they had left the stables, Percy said to the horseman "Got a bit of old tin about anywhere, Eph? Need summat for the boy to bang on." Ephraim scratched his head awhile and then said "There's that old broken swath-turner out in the back yard under they nettles. You could bash one of the wings off ee."

So it was that, ten minutes later, Percy Pound

started up his old Matchless, on the luggage carrier of which he had strapped one of the wings of the swath-turner and a stout iron bar to act as a drumstick. He straddled the low saddle of the big machine, working the hand-throttle so that the engine bellowed in short bursts, while Spider watched, jigging up and down in excitement at the noise.

Then Percy put a hand behind him and patted the pillion seat. "Come on, Spider," he said.

Spider's mouth fell open. Plainly the thought that he was to be offered a ride had not entered his mind. He looked at Percy, he looked at the pillion seat, he looked at the horseman who was standing by, watching.

"Go on, lad," said Ephraim. "Jump on. Percy'll look after thee," and he helped the boy to swing a clumsy leg over, while the foreman reached down either side to plant Spider's boots on the rear footrests.

"Now then, Spider," said Percy, "you put your arms round my middle and you hold on tight," and off they went.

Percy drove slowly out of the yard and up the road to the junction with the drove. Because its rammed chalk surface was rough, he did not increase his speed, but then they came to an opening that led into a large piece of permanent grass, beyond which lay the field called Maggs' Corner. Once on the grass and confident now that the ferocity of the grip round his waist meant Spider would not fall off, he moved through the gears until they were speeding along at a good rate.

Behind him he could hear Spider yelling, not with fear but with delight by the sound of it, and then in front of him he saw a black cloud of birds rise from the new-sown wheat at the sound of the motorcycle.

At the gateway into the field Percy switched off, dismounted and helped the boy down. He unstrapped the piece of tin and the iron rod from the luggage carrier.

"Quiet now," he said to Spider, and put a finger to his lips, and they stood still, waiting, while the birds circled above, and then, at first in ones and twos, and then in numbers, flew down again and pitched further down the field, in which the wheat was just beginning to show green in the drills.

Then Percy gave the rod and the tin to Spider.

"Now then, sojer," he said (for Tom had told him of his subterfuge), "see all the bad birds down there, stealing Mister's corn?" He pointed, and Spider nodded. "Right then," said Percy. "Up and at 'em!" and he swung open the gate.

Then down Maggs' Corner marched the thin figure of Spider Sparrow in his overlarge greatcoat, each foot turned out at forty-five degrees from the straight, banging his piece of tin for all he was worth.

"Geddoff croaks! Bad croaks! Bad uns! Bad uns!" shouted the crowstarver.

❧

Crowstarving was the ideal job for Spider, though he could not have said why, even had he possessed the vocabulary to do so. To begin with, he was on his own, which he liked to be, yet never alone, for all around him were animals of one sort or another. There were the croaks of course, keeping him on the move and requiring him to shout and to bang his tin, both of which things he liked doing. But then in the quiet intervals, when the black thieves had temporarily left to pilfer someone else's corn, there were all sorts of creatures for him to enjoy watching. There were many other sorts of birds, some of which, like wood pigeons, feasted on the sprouting wheat as greedily as had the crows and rooks and jackdaws, but because they were not croaks – and only croaks, he had been told, were bad – Spider allowed them to eat in peace.

At one end of Maggs' Corner (it was a roughly triangular field) there was a small spinney of ash and hawthorn, and here the wood pigeons rested when full-cropped.

"Coo-coo-*roo*, coo-*coo*" – repeatedly they sang these five notes – and soon grew used to hearing them echoed from below in an exact facsimile of their song.

The magpies too, more inquisitive by nature, became accustomed to hearing, coming from the mouth of a human figure, their loud chattering "Chak-chak-chak-chak!"

"Peewit!" cried Spider to the flocks of lapwings that flew over his head, sometimes with their peculiar slow flapping wing-beats, and sometimes throwing themselves wildly about in the air. And there were so many other birds, out there in the wide open spaces under the huge bowl of the sky, that called to the crowstarver and were answered by him.

"Kiu! Kiu! Werro!" barked the little owl, abroad in daylight unlike the rest of his clan.

"Korrk-kok!" crowed the pheasant, and "Krric! Krric! Kar-wic!" grated the partridge, while high above, the skylarks poured down their long-drawn-out high-pitched musical cadenzas. And all were faithfully answered by Spider.

As well as these and many other kinds of birds, there were beasts on Outoverdown Farm, rabbits galore, quite a few hares, the occasional fox, hunting in the daytime.

All of these of course kept well clear of Spider while he was frightening the croaks, but in the quieter intervals of the day he had many creatures to look at. Sometimes they were at a distance, but, as though to compensate for his other deficiencies, his eyesight was exceptionally sharp and his hearing very keen. Some of these animals – like the 'barrits' – Spider knew well, for he had so often seen them before, hopping about the headlands of the fields or popping into burrows at the edge of the drove, but he could not put a name to hare or to fox.

However he had at home a picture book that Tom and Kathie had given him because of his interest in animals, and he would point out to them the likeness of some creature that he had seen and they would tell him its name (for he could not read a word). Thus after seeing a hare lolloping across Maggs' Corner one day, he found it in his book, showed it to them, and said "Big barrit?"

"No," they said. "Hare."

Spider looked puzzled. He put his hand up to his head and pulled at his forelock.

"No," said Kathie. "It's spelled different."

Not understanding, Spider said again "Big barrit?"

Tom nodded. "All right," he said. "You call it that, son, if you like. We'll know what you mean."

Then, a day or two later, Spider saw a fox. He was

sitting in the edge of the spinney, eating his lunch. Maggs' Corner was for the moment free of croaks, and only the privileged wood pigeons filled their crops. Suddenly they too all lifted off and flew hurriedly away, and Spider, looking in that direction, saw a red-coated bushy-tailed figure trotting along the headland of the field towards him.

He sat quite still, even ceasing to chew, as the animal came nearer. Suddenly it saw him and stopped in its tracks, one fore-paw raised.

Then a truly surprising thing happened. The fox came on, more slowly now, alert but showing no sign of fear, until it was no more than ten feet from the boy, and then it sat down facing him, ears pricked, eyes fixed upon him. It licked its lips. "Good un!" said Spider softly, and he broke off a bit of bread and awkwardly, for all his actions tended to be clumsy, tossed it towards this wild animal, which by rights should have fled at the mere sight of him and would surely have done so from any other human being.

Patently, by some strange instinct, the fox seemed to know that this human was different from others and posed no sort of threat. It moved in a step or two and picked up the bread. It did not gulp it down or make off with it, as it would have done had danger threatened, but ate it delicately, like a cat. The bread finished, fox and boy remained quite still, each gazing into the other's eyes, and then, unhurriedly, the animal turned and trotted back in the direction from which it had come.

That night Spider got out his picture book and found a portrait of a fox. Excitedly, he showed it to his parents, grinning and pointing. "Spider see!" he said.

"Saw a fox, did you?" they said.

"Vox!" said Spider. "Vox! Good un!" and he pointed to his mouth and made chewing movements.

"Eating summat, was it?" asked Tom.

"Or was it when you were eating your lunch?" asked Kathie. To both questions Spider nodded vigorously, and then he performed a little pantomime for them.

First, he put a hand to a pocket, pretending to draw something out and break a piece off it. Then he carried one hand to his mouth and, breaking off another imaginary piece, stretched out his arm and offered it to Mollie.

"Spider eat, vox eat," he said.

"Sharing his lunch with a fox?" said Kathie later when Spider had gone to bed. "Whoever heard tell of such a thing! Dunno what goes on inside his head."

"Dunno what Mister'd say if t'was true!" said Tom. "Only good fox for him is a dead one."

"What does Mister say about Spider?" asked Kathie. "D'you reckon he thinks he's doing the job all right?"

"Too true," said Tom. "Couple of days after he'd started, I was feeding the rams in that long paddock by the roadside, you know, and I heard a clip-clop and Mister comes riding down the road, and he pulls Sturdiboy up and says to me 'How's that boy of yours getting on, Tom? Mister Pound tells me he's put him up on Maggs' Corner. Keeping the birds off, is he?'

"Well, before I could answer, our Spider starts up. Now, Maggs' Corner's a good half mile from the rams' paddock, I reckon, but you could hear him a-hollering and a-banging as though he was tother side of the fence. And we looked up over that way and you could see a great cloud of birds lift off. And Mister looks at me and he grins and he says 'He's doing all right, Tom. That row would wake the dead'."

Spider spent a week or so more up at Maggs' Corner, by which time the wheat was up and getting away strongly and the threat of bird damage had lessened, but on most of those days he came home and acted out his pantomime of feeding the 'vox', so that any belief his parents might have had in this story waned and died, and they thought the whole business to be of his imagination.

Little did they guess that the fox, despite all the racket that Spider made for most of the day, had come again at the boy's lunch time. Each time it came a little nearer to where he sat, until, on his final day of crowstarving on that particular field, it sat before him.

Slowly, Spider stretched out his arm and, gently, the fox took the food from his hand.

Black Beauty

by Anna Sewell

*Black Beauty's happy childhood ends when his mistress
gets sick and he has to be sold. After several new homes,
where he is badly treated and suffers much hardship, he
ends up in London as a cab horse. His master, Jerry, is a
good man, and Black Beauty (now called Jack) makes a
new friend, an old war horse called Captain...*

I saw a great deal of trouble amongst the horses in
London, and much of it that might have been
prevented by a little common sense. We horses do not
mind hard work if we are treated reasonably; and I am
sure there are many driven by quite poor men who have
a happier life than I had when I used to go in the
Countess of W-'s carriage, with my silver-mounted
harness and high feeding.

It often went to my heart to see how the little
ponies were used, straining along with heavy loads, or
staggering under heavy blows from some low cruel boy.
Once I saw a little grey pony with a thick mane and a
pretty head, and so much like Merrylegs, that if I had
not been in harness, I should have neighed to him. He

was doing his best to pull a heavy cart, while a strong rough boy was cutting him under the belly with his whip, and chucking cruelly at his little mouth. Could it be Merrylegs? It was just like him; but then Mr Blomefield was never to sell him, and I think he would not do it; but this might have been quite as good a little fellow, and had as happy a place when he was young.

I often noticed the great speed at which butchers' horses were made to go, though I did not know why it was so, till one day when we had to wait some time in St John's Wood. There was a butcher's shop next door, and, as we were standing, a butcher's cart came dashing up at a great pace. The horse was hot, and much exhausted; he hung his head down, while his heaving sides and trembling legs showed how hard he had been driven. The lad jumped out of the cart and was getting the basket, when the master came out of the shop much displeased. After looking at the horse, he turned angrily to the lad:

"How many times shall I tell you not to drive in this way? You ruined the last horse and broke his wind, and you are going to ruin this in the same way. If you were not my own son, I would dismiss you on the spot; it is a disgrace to have a horse brought to the shop in a condition like that; you are liable to be taken up by the police for such driving, and if you are, you need not look to me for bail, for I have spoken to you till I am tired; you must look out for yourself."

During this speech, the boy had stood by, sullen and dogged, but when his father ceased, he broke out angrily. It wasn't his fault, and he wouldn't take the blame, he was only going by orders all the time.

"You always say, 'Now be quick; now look sharp!' and when I go to the houses, one wants a leg of mutton for an early dinner, and I must be back with it in a quarter of an hour. Another cook had forgotten to order the beef; I must go and fetch it and be back in no time, or the mistress will scold; and the housekeeper says they have company coming unexpectedly and must have some chops sent up directly; and the lady at No. 4, in the Crescent, *never* orders her dinner till the meat comes in for lunch, and it's nothing but hurry, hurry, all the time. If the gentry would think of what they want, and order their meat the day before, there need not be this blow up!"

"I wish to goodness they would," said the butcher; "'twould save me a wonderful deal of harass, and I could suit my customers much better if I knew beforehand – but there – what's the use of talking – who ever thinks of a butcher's convenience, or a butcher's horse? Now then, take him in, and look to him well: mind, he does not go out again today, and if anything else is wanted, you must carry it yourself in the basket." With that he went in, and the horse was led away.

But all boys are not cruel. I have seen some as fond of their pony or donkey as if it had been a favourite dog, and the little creatures have worked away as cheerfully and willingly for their young drivers as I work for Jerry. It may be hard work sometimes, but a friend's hand and voice make it easy.

There was a young coster-boy who came up our street with greens and potatoes; he had an old pony, not very handsome, but the cheerfullest and pluckiest little thing I ever saw, and to see how fond those two were of each other, was a treat. The pony followed his master like a dog, and when he got into his cart, would trot off without a whip or a word, and rattle down the street as merrily as if he had come out of the Queen's stables. Jerry liked the boy, and called him 'Prince Charlie', for he said he would make a king of drivers some day.

There was an old man, too, who used to come up our street with a little coal cart; he wore a coalheaver's hat, and looked rough and black. He and his old horse used to plod together along the street, like two good partners who understood each other; the horse would stop of his own accord, at the doors where they took coal off him; he used to keep one ear bent towards his master. The old man's cry could be heard up the street long before he came near. I never knew what he said, but the children called him 'Old Ba-a-ar Hoo', for it sounded like that. Polly took her coal off him, and was very friendly, and Jerry said it was a comfort to think how happy an old horse *might* be in a poor place.

&

As we came into the yard one afternoon, Polly came out: "Jerry! I've had Mr B– here asking about your vote, and he wants to hire your cab for the election; he will call for an answer."

"Well, Polly, you may say that my cab will be otherwise engaged; I should not like to have it pasted over with their great bills, and as to make Jack and Captain race about to the public-houses to bring up half-drunken voters, why I think 'twould be an insult to the horses. No, I shan't do it."

"I suppose you'll vote for the gentleman? He said he was of your politics."

"So he is in some things, but I shall not vote for him, Polly; you know what his trade is?"

"Yes."

"Well, a man who gets rich by that trade, may be all very well in some ways, but he is blind as to what working men want: I could not in my conscience send him up to make the laws. I dare say they'll be angry, but every man must do what he thinks to be the best for his country."

On the morning before the election, Jerry was putting me into the shafts, when Dolly came into the yard, sobbing and crying, with her little blue frock and white pinafore spattered all over with mud.

"Why, Dolly, what is the matter?"

"Those naughty boys," she sobbed, "have thrown the dirt all over me, and called me a little ragga – ragga –"

"They called her a little blue raggamuffin, father," said Harry, who ran in looking very angry; "but I have given it to them, they won't insult my sister again. I have given them a thrashing they will remember; a set of cowardly, rascally, orange blackguards!"

Jerry kissed the child and said, "Run in to mother, my pet, and tell her I think you had better stay at home today and help her."

Then turning gravely to Harry:

"My boy, I hope you will always defend your sister, and give anybody who insults her a good thrashing – that is as it should be; but mind, I won't have any election blackguarding on my premises. There are as many blue blackguards as there are orange, and as many white as there are purple, or any other colour, and

I won't have any of my family mixed up with it. Even women and children are ready to quarrel for the sake of a colour, and not one in ten of them knows what it is about."

"Why, father, I thought blue was for Liberty."

"My boy, Liberty does not come from colours; they only show party, and all the liberty you can get out of them is liberty to get drunk at other people's expense, liberty to ride to the poll in a dirty old cab, liberty to abuse anyone that does not wear your colour, and to shout yourself hoarse at what you only half understand – that's your liberty!"

"Oh, father, you are laughing."

"No, Harry, I am serious, and I am ashamed to see how men go on that ought to know better. An election is a very serious thing; at least it ought to be, and every man ought to vote according to his conscience, and let his neighbour do the same."

༄

At last came the election day; there was no lack of work for Jerry and me. First came a stout puffy gentleman with a carpet bag; he wanted to go to the Bishopsgate Station; then we were called by a party who wished to be taken to the Regent's Park; and next we were wanted in a side street where a timid anxious old lady was waiting to be taken to the bank: there we had to stop to take her back again, and just as we had set her down, a red-faced gentleman with a handful of papers came running up out of breath, and before Jerry could get down, he had opened the door, popped himself in, and called out, "Bow Street Police Station, quick!", so off we went with him, and when after another turn or two we came back, there was no other cab on the stand. Jerry put on my nose-bag, for as he said, "We must eat when we can on such days as these; so munch away, Jack, and make the best of your time, old boy."

I found I had a good feed of crushed oats wetted up with a little bran; this would be a treat any day, but was specially refreshing then. Jerry was so thoughtful and kind – what horse would not do his best for such a master? Then he took out one of Polly's meat pies, and standing near me, he began to eat it. The streets were very full, and the cabs with the Candidates' colours on them were dashing about through the crowd as if life and limb were of no consequence; we saw two people knocked down that day, and one was a woman. The horses were having a bad time of it, poor things! but the voters inside thought nothing of that, many of them were half drunk, hurrahing out of the cab windows if their own party came by. It was the first election I had seen, and I don't want to be in another, though I have heard things are better now.

Jerry and I had not eaten many mouthfuls before a poor young woman, carrying a heavy child, came along the street. She was looking this way, and that way, and seemed quite bewildered. Presently she made her way up to Jerry, and asked if he could tell her the way to St Thomas's Hospital, and how far it was to get there. She had come from the country that morning, she said, in a market cart; she did not know about the election and was quite a stranger in London. She had got an order for the Hospital for her little boy. The child was crying with a feeble pining cry.

"Poor little fellow!" she said, "he suffers a deal of

185

pain; he is four years old and can't walk any more than a baby; but the doctor said if I could get him into the Hospital, he might get well; pray, sir, how far is it? And which way is it?"

"Why, missis," said Jerry, "you can't get there walking through crowds like this! Why, it is three miles away, and that child is heavy."

"Yes, bless him, he is, but I am strong, thank God, and if I knew the way, I think I should get on somehow: please tell me the way."

"You can't do it," said Jerry, "you might be knocked down and the child be run over. Now, look here, just get into this cab, and I'll drive you safe to the hospital: don't you see the rain is coming on?"

"No, sir, no, I can't do that, thank you, I have only just money enough to get back with: please tell me the way."

"Look you here, missis," said Jerry, "I've got a wife and dear children at home, and I know a father's feelings: now get you into that cab, and I'll take you there for nothing; I'd be ashamed of myself to let a woman and a sick child run a risk like that."

"Heaven bless you!" said the woman, bursting into tears.

"There, there, cheer up, my dear, I'll soon take you there; let me put you inside."

As Jerry went to open the door, two men, with colours in their hats and button-holes, ran up, calling out, "Cab!"

"Engaged," cried Jerry; but one of the men, pushing past the woman, sprang into the cab, followed by the other. Jerry looked as stern as a policeman: "This cab is already engaged, gentlemen, by that lady."

"Lady!" said one of them; "oh! she can wait: our business is very important, besides we were in first, it is our right, and we shall stay in."

A droll smile came over Jerry's face as he shut the door upon them. "All right, gentlemen, pray stay in as long as it suits you: I can wait whilst you rest yourselves," and turning his back upon them, he walked up to the young woman, who was standing near me. "They'll soon be gone," he said, laughing, "don't trouble yourself, my dear."

And they soon were gone, for when they understood Jerry's dodge, they got out, calling him all sorts of bad names, and blustering about his number, and getting a summons. After this little stoppage we were soon on our way to the hospital, going as much as possible through by-streets. Jerry rung the great bell, and helped the young woman out.

"Thank you a thousand times," she said; "I could never have got here alone."

"You're kindly welcome, and I hope the dear child will soon be better."

He watched her go in at the door, and gently he said to himself, "Inasmuch as ye have done it to one of the least of these." Then he patted my neck, which was always his way when anything pleased him.

The rain was now coming down fast, and just as we were leaving the hospital the door opened again, and the porter called out, "Cab!" We stopped, and a lady came down the steps. Jerry seemed to know her at once; she put back her veil and said, "Barker! Jeremiah Barker! Is it you? I am very glad to find you here; you are just the friend I want, for it is very difficult to get a cab in this part of London today."

"I shall be proud to serve you, ma'am, I am right glad I happened to be here; where may I take you to, ma'am?"

"To the Paddington Station, and then if we are in good time, as I think we shall be, you shall tell me all about Mary and the children."

We got to the station in good time, and, being under shelter, the lady stood a good while talking to Jerry. I found she had been Polly's mistress, and after many inquiries about her, she said:

"How do you find the cab work suits you in winter? I know Mary was rather anxious about you last year."

"Yes, ma'am, she was; I had a bad cough that followed me up quite into the warm weather, and when

I am kept out late, she does worry herself a good deal. You see, ma'am, it is all hours and all weathers, and that does try a man's constitution; but I am getting on pretty well, and I should feel quite lost if I had not horses to look after. I was brought up to it, and I am afraid I should not do so well at anything else."

"Well, Barker," she said, "it would be a great pity that you should seriously risk your health in this work, not only for your own, but for Mary and the children's sake: there are many places where good drivers or good grooms are wanted; and if ever you think you ought to give up this cab work, let me know." Then, sending some kind messages to Mary, she put something into his hand, saying, "There is five shillings each for the two children; Mary will know how to spend it."

Jerry thanked her and seemed much pleased, and, turning out of the station, we at last reached home, and I, at least, was tired.

∝

Captain and I were great friends. He was a noble old fellow, and he was very good company. I never thought that he would have to leave his home and go down the hill, but his turn came; and this was how it happened. I was not there, but I heard all about it.

He and Jerry had taken a party to the great railway station over London Bridge, and were coming back, somewhere between the Bridge and the Monument, when Jerry saw a brewer's empty dray coming along, drawn by two powerful horses. The drayman was lashing his horses with his heavy whip; the dray was light, and they started off at a furious rate; the man had no control over them, and the street was full of traffic;

one young girl was knocked down and run over, and the next moment they dashed up against our cab; both the wheels were torn off, and the cab was thrown over. Captain was dragged down, the shafts splintered, and one of them ran into his side. Jerry too was thrown, but was only bruised; nobody could tell how he escaped, he always said 'twas a miracle. When poor Captain was got up, he was found to be very much cut and knocked about. Jerry led him home gently, and a sad sight it was to see the blood soaking into his white coat, and dropping from his side and shoulder. The drayman was proved to be very drunk, and was fined, and the brewer had to pay damages to our master; but there was no one to pay damages to poor Captain.

The farrier and Jerry did the best they could to ease his pain, and make him comfortable. The fly had to be mended, and for several days I did not go out, and Jerry earned nothing.

At first Captain seemed to do well, but he was a very old horse, and it was only his wonderful constitution, and Jerry's care, that had kept him up at the cab-work so long; now he broke down very much. The farrier said he might mend up enough to sell for a few pounds, but Jerry said, no! a few pounds got by selling a good old servant into hard work, and misery, would canker all the rest of his money, and he thought the kindest thing he could do for the fine old fellow would be to put a sure bullet through his heart, and then he would never suffer more; for he did not know where to find a kind master for the rest of his days.

The day after this was decided, Harry took me to the forge for some new shoes; when I returned, Captain was gone. I and the family all felt it very much.

Jerry had now to look out for another horse, and he soon heard of one through an acquaintance who was under-groom in a nobleman's stables. He was a valuable young horse, but he had run away, smashed into another carriage, flung his lordship out, and so cut and blemished himself that he was no longer fit for a gentleman's stables, and the coachman had orders to look round, and sell him as well as he could.

"I can do with high spirits," said Jerry, "if a horse is not vicious or hard-mouthed."

"There is not a bit of vice in him," said the man, "his mouth is very tender, and I think myself that was the cause of the accident; you see he had just been clipped, and the weather was bad, and he had not had exercise enough, and when he did go out, he was as full of spring as a balloon. Our governor (the coachman, I mean) had him harnessed in as tight and strong as he could, with the martingale, and the bearing rein, a very sharp curb, and the reins put in at the bottom bar; it is my belief that it made the horse mad, being tender in the mouth and so full of spirit."

"Likely enough; I'll come and see him," said Jerry.

The next day, Hotspur – that was his name – came home; he was a fine brown horse, without a white hair in him, as tall as Captain, with a very handsome head, and only five years old. I gave him a friendly greeting by way of good fellowship, but did not ask him any questions. The first night he was very restless; instead of lying down, he kept jerking his halter rope up and down through the ring, and knocking the block about against the manger so that I could not sleep. However, the next day, after five or six hours in the cab, he came in quiet and sensible. Jerry patted and talked to him a good deal, and very soon they understood each other, and Jerry said that with an easy bit, and plenty of work, he would be as gentle as a lamb; and that it was an ill wind that blew nobody good, for if his lordship had lost a hundred-guinea favourite, the cabman had gained a good horse with all his strength in him.

Hotspur thought it a great come down to be a cab-horse, and was disgusted at standing in the rank, but he confessed to me at the end of the week that an easy mouth, and a free hand, made up for a great deal, and after all, the work was not so degrading as having one's head and tail fastened to each other at the saddle. In fact, he settled in well, and Jerry liked him very much.

❧

Christmas and the New Year are very merry times for some people; but for cabmen and cabmen's horses it is no holiday, though it may be a harvest. There are so many parties, balls, and places of amusement open, that the work is hard and often late. Sometimes driver and horse have to wait for hours in the rain or frost, shivering with cold, whilst the merry people within are dancing away to the music. I wonder if the beautiful ladies ever think of the weary cabman waiting on his box, and his patient beast standing, till his legs get stiff with cold.

I had now most of the evening work, as I was well accustomed to standing, and Jerry was also more afraid of Hotspur taking cold. We had a great deal of late work in the Christmas week, and Jerry's cough was bad; but however late we were, Polly sat up for him, and came out with the lantern to meet him, looking anxious and troubled.

On the evening of the New Year, we had to take two gentlemen to a house in one of the West End squares. We set them down at nine o'clock and were told to come again at eleven. "But," said one of them, "as it is a card party, you may have to wait a few minutes, but don't be late."

As the clock struck eleven we were at the door, for Jerry was always punctual. The clock chimed the quarters – one, two, three, and then struck twelve, but the door did not open.

The wind had been very changeable, with squalls of rain during the day, but now it came on a sharp driving sleet, which seemed to come all the way round; it was very cold, and there was no shelter. Jerry got off his box and came and pulled one of my cloths a little more over my neck; then he took a turn or two up and down, stamping his feet; then he began to beat his arms, but that set him off coughing; so he opened the cab door and sat at the bottom with his feet on the pavement, and was a little sheltered. Still the clock chimed the quarters, and no one came. At half-past twelve, he rang the bell and asked the servant if he would be wanted that night.

"Oh! yes, you'll be wanted safe enough," said the man, "you must not go, it will soon be over," and again Jerry sat down, but his voice was so hoarse I could hardly hear him.

At a quarter past one the door opened, and the two gentlemen came out; they got into the cab without a word, and told Jerry where to drive, that was nearly two miles. My legs were numb with cold, and I thought I should have stumbled. When the men got out, they never said they were sorry to have kept us waiting so long, but were angry at the charge: however, as Jerry never charged more than was his due, so he never took less, and they had to pay for the two hours and a quarter waiting; but it was hard-earned money to Jerry.

At last we got home; he could hardly speak, and his cough was dreadful. Polly asked no questions, but opened the door and held the lantern for him.

"Can't I do something?" she said.

"Yes, get Jack something warm, and then boil me some gruel."

This was said in a hoarse whisper; he could hardly get his breath, but he gave me a rub down as usual, and even went up into the hayloft for an extra bundle of straw for my bed. Polly brought me a warm mash that made me comfortable, and then they locked the door.

It was late the next morning before any one came, and then it was only Harry. He cleaned us and fed us, and swept out the stalls, then he put the straw back again as if it was Sunday. He was very still, and neither whistled nor sang. At noon he came again, and gave us our food and water: this time Dolly came with him; she was crying, and I could gather from what they said that Jerry was dangerously ill, and the doctor said it was a bad case. So two days passed, and there was great trouble indoors. We only saw Harry and sometimes Dolly. I think she came for company, for Polly was always with Jerry, and he had to be kept very quiet.

On the third day, whilst Harry was in the stable, a tap came at the door, and Governor Grant came in.

"I wouldn't go to the house, my boy," he said, "but I want to know how your father is."

"He is very bad," said Harry, "he can't be much worse; they call it 'bronchitis'; the doctor thinks it will turn one way or another tonight."

"That's bad, very bad!" said Grant, shaking his head; "I know two men who died of that last week; it takes 'em off in no time; but whilst there's life there's hope, so you must keep up your spirits."

"Yes," said Harry, quickly, "and the doctor said that father had a better chance than most men, because he didn't drink. He said yesterday the fever was so high that if father had been a drinking man, it would have burnt him up like a piece of paper; but I believe he thinks he will get over it; don't you think he will, Mr Grant?"

The Governor looked puzzled.

"If there's any rule that good men should get over these things, I am sure he will, my boy; he's the best man I know. I'll look in early tomorrow."

Early next morning he was there.

"Well?" said he.

"Father is better," said Harry. "Mother hopes he will get over it."

"Thank God!" said the Governor, "and now you must keep him warm, and keep his mind easy, and that brings me to the horses; you see, Jack will be all the better for the rest of a week or two in a warm stable, and you can easily take him a turn up and down the street to stretch his legs; but this young one, if he does not get work, he will soon be all up on end, as you may say, and will be rather too much for you; and when he does go out, there'll be an accident."

"It is like that now," said Harry. "I have kept him short of corn, but he's so full of spirit I don't know what to do with him."

"Just so," said Grant. "Now look here, will you tell your mother that, if she is agreeable, I will come for him every day till something is arranged, and take him for a good spell of work, and whatever he earns I'll bring your mother half of it, and that will help with the horses' feed. Your father is in a good club, I know, but that won't keep the horses, and they'll be eating their heads off all this time; I'll come at noon and hear what she says," and without waiting for Harry's thanks, he was gone.

At noon I think he went and saw Polly, for he and Harry came to the stable together, harnessed Hotspur and took him out.

For a week or more he came for Hotspur, and when Harry thanked him or said anything about his kindness he laughed it off, saying it was all good luck for him, for his horses were wanting a little rest which they would not otherwise have had.

Jerry grew better, steadily, but the doctor said that he must never go back to the cab work again if he wished to be an old man. The children had many consultations together about what father and mother would do, and how they could help to earn money.

One afternoon, Hotspur was brought in very wet and dirty.

"The streets are nothing but slush," said the Governor; "it will give you a good warming, my boy, to get him clean and dry."

"All right, Governor," said Harry, "I shall not leave him till he is; you know I have been trained by my father."

"I wish all the boys had been trained like you," said the Governor.

While Harry was sponging off the mud from Hotspur's body and legs, Dolly came in, looking very full of something.

"Who lives at Fairstowe, Harry? Mother has got a letter from Fairstowe; she seemed so glad, and ran upstairs to father with it."

"Don't you know? Why, it is the name of Mrs Fowler's place – mother's old mistress, you know – the lady that father met last summer, who sent you and me five shillings each."

"Oh! Mrs Fowler; of course I know all about her. I wonder what she is writing to mother about."

"Mother wrote to her last week," said Harry; "you know she told father if ever he gave up the cab work, she would like to know. I wonder what she says; run in and see, Dolly."

Harry scrubbed away at Hotspur with a huish! huish! like any old ostler.

In a few minutes Dolly came dancing into the stable.

"Oh! Harry, there never was anything so beautiful; Mrs Fowler says we are all to go and live near her. There is a cottage new empty that will just suit us, with a garden, and a hen house, and apple trees, and everything! and her coachman is going away in the spring, and then she will want father in his place; and there are good families round where you can get a place in the garden, or the stable, or as a page boy; and there's a good school for me; and mother is laughing and crying by turns, and father does look so happy!"

"That's uncommon jolly," said Harry, "and just the right thing, I should say; it will suit father and mother both; but I don't intend to be a page boy with tight clothes and rows of buttons. I'll be a groom or a gardener."

It was quickly settled that as soon as Jerry was well enough they should remove to the country, and that the cab and horses should be sold as soon as possible.

This was heavy news for me, for I was not young now, and could not look for any improvement in my condition. Since I left Birtwick I had never been so happy as with my dear master, Jerry; but three years of cab work, even under the best conditions, will tell on one's strength, and I felt that I was not the horse that I had been.

Grant said at once that he would take Hotspur; and there were men on the stand who would have bought me; but Jerry said I should not go to cab work again with just anybody, and the Governor promised to find a place for me where I should be comfortable.

The day came for going away. Jerry had not been allowed to go out yet, and I never saw him after that New Year's Eve. Polly and the children came to bid me good-bye. "Poor old Jack! Dear old Jack! I wish we could take you with us," she said, and then, laying her hand on my mane, she put her face close to my neck and kissed me. Dolly was crying and kissed me too. Harry stroked me a great deal, but said nothing, only he seemed very sad, and so I was led away to my new place.

Poor Arthur

by Gene Kemp

After Dennis, the cat, had caught the white mouse one day when the cage was being cleaned out – by Bloggs, my stupid sister, of course – I wouldn't have let it happen, only she's so slow, she didn't see Dennis coming like a streak of death across the floor, up on to the table, and to where that white mouse was just running round and round, then Mum said there weren't to be any more animals, because she couldn't stand the smell, and she was the only one who fed them.

Well, we took to moaning about having no animals except the cat, Dennis, you remember, and he's so old I'm sure he was never a kitten, and always asleep except when he's hunting defenceless birds and mice, and being all streaky and murderous, and then we took to hanging around pet shops and looking at the creatures. I fancied a yellow spotted snake and Bloggs a Great Dane, but we didn't have much hope of either, really, not with our mum.

Then, just at the right moment, our next door neighbour said she'd got gerbils, and they were very nice, and you didn't have to clean them out often as they didn't smell.

"All animals smell," said Mum.

The next door neighbour took us all round to the gerbillery, I suppose you could call it, as there were two couples and two sets of baby gerbils.

"I'll give you one for your birthday," she said, as I stood there letting them run over me, with my inside swimming with joy at the feel of their fur and their little soft claws. And Mum said all right then, provided you look after them, not me.

So we cleaned up the old mouse cage, then rushed off to buy sawdust and gerbil food.

And so came Chuchi.

Not that we called her Chuchi at first. We tried Polly, and Nosey and Cleo, but nothing fitted. She wasn't much to look at, a bit tatty, really, with ruffled fur and a big hooked nose which she poked into everything. But she had bright black eyes and she ran to us whenever we came near, head cocked on one side, chattering furiously, hiding nuts, eating nuts, tearing up toilet rolls, kicking angrily with her back feet when she was in a temper. Dad called her the little rat. He was always chatting to her or tempting her with peanuts so that she'd jump really high. Even Mum took to her. She let me have her in my bedroom because the cage didn't smell, and at night I'd let her run round my bed and snuggle in my pyjama pocket.

And she still hadn't got a name.

Then one day Mum said, out of the blue, "Let's go and get some grass seeds for Chuchi. She likes grass seeds."

"Chuchi?"

"Yes. Chuchi, of course." As if we ought to have known all along. "That's the sound we make when we want her to come to us, and it's her funny chatter noise as well."

So there she was. Chuchi. Named at last.

Now all this time we'd kept an eye on Dennis, that hunting cat. There was no smell to tempt him, but he knew something very interesting was going on. Dennis is a clever cat. He watches and waits. Sometimes we'd find him outside my room, washing himself very innocently. Chuchi grew bad tempered. Straw and shredded toilet rolls flew through the air.

"She needs a mate," Dad announced at tea time.

"Babies!" Bloggs cried, stupid eyes shining.

"I like Chuchi, but enough is enough," said Mum.

"Females need mating," said Dad. "That's why she's irritable. Females do get irritable."

"Humph," snorted Mum, banging down scrambled eggs on to the table. I thought for a minute she was going to bang them on his head.

❧

We bought another gerbil.

Dad built a second cage in case they didn't get on, and for the babies later.

This turned out to be a good thing, because Chuchi took a violent dislike to the new gerbil, and chased him out of the cage, biting and kicking like fury. He was terrified and squealed pitifully, poor little thing, only half her size. We called him Arthur. The next day we tried to put him in with Chuchi again, but it was no good. The cage was her territory and she wasn't having Arthur in it.

201

Then Dad thought of putting the cages next to each other, and soon they were sniffing each other through the wire.

A week later they were both living happily in Chuchi's cage. Arthur grew bigger and braver, but she was still the boss. They looked very alike now, though Chuchi still had the longer tail and the bigger nose, and a more untidy look.

Dennis the hunter waited, licking his tabby fur. Patient, wicked Dennis.

"I do wish she'd have babies," sighed Bloggs.

"Well, she's getting fatter," said Mum.

❧

My dad drives a bus, and works different shifts. That day he'd gone to work very early, returned at ten in the morning, and gone out again at three. We came home with Mum, who's a teacher, at four. There was a note for us on the table. Dad in a temper is like Vesuvius erupting. The note said:

"If I find out who left the cage door open this morning, you'll wish you'd never been born, for that murdering cat has killed Chuchi. I've tried to catch him but he was too fast, which is just as well for him."

He'd put her on the sideboard, and she was stiff and cold, but her fur was as soft as ever. Mum was sobbing, and tears were streaming down Bloggs's face. I didn't cry. I just stood there, stroking her over and over again.

"We must bury her," Mum said, at last.

I found a Dinky car container with a transparent top, and Bloggs put her inside, wrapped in cotton wool. Mum fetched some little flowers from the garden and put them in with her, and Bloggs drew a cross on a card and wrote: 'Here lies Chuchi, the Beloved.'

We dug a hole and placed her inside. The ground was hard. It hadn't rained for a long time.

Dad came home, face pale, anger gone. "I loved the little rat," he said.

Mum stirred. "We ought to go and see if Arthur's all right. He must have been terrified when Dennis came out of nowhere and seized Chuchi."

We all trooped up to my bedroom, and Arthur was there, nervous and jittery; not surprisingly.

Bloggs felt in the dark room Dad had built on above the cage, as a nursery, still crying. "Now, there'll never be any babies," and then: "I can feel something. There's something here. The babies!"

"Let me see!" we all cried.

But we couldn't, for it had been made specially dark

and quiet for the babies and the only way to see inside was to take the top off.

I fetched the screwdriver. Dad unscrewed the screws. Bloggs chewed her fingers. It seemed to take hours, but at last, there they lay, naked, pink, squirming, beautiful, four of them.

"But how can they survive," Mum whispered, "without Chuchi to feed them? I can't feed anything as small as that. They'll starve."

Dad's face had turned even paler. Bloggs was crying again.

"No, I'll put them to sleep, first," he said.

At that moment Arthur jumped out of my hand, where I'd been stroking him for comfort, and ran across the room. We watched him. Perhaps Bloggs isn't so stupid as I've been saying all along, for she understood first.

"Look! Look! That's not Arthur! The tail's too long and the nose is too big, and he's... She's heading for the babies! Dennis killed *Arthur*, not Chuchi! It's Chuchi! She's alive!"

Chuchi had reached the cage and the babies. She pulled them to her, and then all her blue and pink toilet paper, covered herself and the babies with it, and sat, glaring out of the heap, very angrily indeed, as if she didn't think much of us.

We were all grinning from ear to ear.

"Everything's going to be all right. The babies will live now."

"I'll put the roof back on so that they can be quiet," said Dad.

As he screwed in the screws, he started to laugh,

a funny sort of laugh.

"What is it, Dad?"

"It's just that, well, poor old Arthur – he didn't have much of a life because Chuchi bullied him all the time, and when he dies he gets buried with someone else's name over him, and all of us smiling and happy because he's dead and not Chuchi. Poor old Arthur, I say."

"Poor Arthur," we all echoed, but we still didn't feel sad. Chuchi and the babies were going to live. Everything would be all right. Except for Arthur. Poor Arthur.

Stories from Firefly Island

by Ben Blathwayt

On warm nights the animals of Firefly Island would gather on the beach at the edge of the forest and ask Tortoise for a story. Tortoise had many memories and many stories.

"Tell us why the frogs croak at night," they would say. "Tell us the story of Lizard's race and of the great storm; about the Big Bottle-nose and Brave Pig."

Tortoise was wise, Tortoise knew almost everything. "What is the moon?" the animals sometimes asked. "What are the stars? Tell us why we are here, and where we come from."

Tortoise would blink and take a while to answer. He was old, very old, but not old enough to know that their island had once been molten rock and bare of any life at all, that the sea had risen and fallen many times, that the land had joined and unjoined. Tortoise had not been here to see the first seeds and nuts arrive, blown on the wind or carried by tides. Grasses, bushes and trees had sprouted from sand-filled cracks in the rock, and eventually insects and birds came to their branches.

Tortoise could tell them only that their ancestors had always been here; that the island was all there was upon the sea; that the sea itself stretched flat, the same for ever and ever, and the sky, too, spread outwards endless and empty.

Tortoise supposed the moon was a cluster of glow-worms and each star a bright firefly asleep on the blackness of the night: surely this was how it was – and it would always be the same.

The animals loved Tortoise. "Tell us another story," they said.

"About us!" giggled the monkeys. "Tell a story about us."

Tortoise frowned, the other animals sighed, for monkeys meant trouble. But Tortoise told them a story…

❧

Many years ago there was a terrible storm, a storm that rocked every branch of every tree and sent waves foaming into the fringe of the forest itself.

With the whistle of the wind howling right through the night, and the rain lashing every hole and crevice, none of the island's animals got any sleep at all.

By morning they were exhausted. The storm died away, the sea grew calm, the sun came out and the whole forest steamed. Every bird and creature dried itself and then fell thankfully asleep, a long deep sleep that lasted until sunset.

Now, while most of the animals were still tired enough at the end of that day of recovery to settle down as usual for a good night's rest – the monkeys were NOT. They felt completely refreshed. They swung through the branches and hooted and howled and chattered and joked. What a noise! They carried on like this until dawn, so that nobody else on the whole island got any rest at all. And the following day, of course, they fell asleep in the hot sun, while the other animals had to busy themselves in their daily search for food.

And when did those monkeys wake up again? Just as the sun went down.

It became a dreadful habit: they slept by day and played by night. The storm had upset the rhythm of the island. The monkeys just laughed when the others begged them to be quiet.

It was all very well for the monkeys: they managed to grab fruit as they swung through the trees; even with a thin moon they could see well enough. *They* didn't go hungry. But the birds couldn't fly at night and it was too dark for some of the animals, too cold for others. Day was the time to feed, night was the time to sleep – it had always been that way.

"What are we going to do?" the animals asked each other in desperation. They settled down to think of a plan.

The finches suddenly had an idea. They told Grass-snake and Lizard. The chipmunks and porcupines agreed; so did the deer and the wild pigs. Everyone thought it a very good plan, everyone except the frogs who no one had bothered to tell. The frogs seemed to get left out of everything – perhaps because they lived in far-off wet and boggy places where nobody else wanted to go.

Wild Pig asked the finches: "When are we going to have this concert?"

"Tomorrow," said the finches, "at sunrise."

The next morning, full of fruit and tired out from their night of fooling about, the monkeys settled down to sleep. The sun was warm, how peaceful they felt.

Then the finches gave the signal to begin. Already gathered beneath the trees where the monkeys slept, every creature on the island began to sing. If they couldn't sing, then they began to squeak, to snort, to bellow, or to grunt. The leaves of the trees shook with the noise of it all. The monkeys woke and held on tightly to their branches. At first they didn't know what was happening. The singing echoed from cliff top to tree top and back again.

"Quiet please!" shrieked the monkeys. "We're tired, we want to sleep!"

But the animals' concert went on. It was no use the monkeys blocking their ears or moving to a further tree; the orchestra of animals followed below them.

"Please let us rest," begged the monkeys, "it's been a long night, we need our sleep." But the chorus of voices kept singing and the pelicans brought fruit and water for dry throats.

"How long is this going to go on?" groaned the monkeys. All day, thought the finches to themselves, but they said nothing.

လ

And that's just how long the concert lasted – all day. Towards sunset the noise grew wilder, more ragged and disorganised. But no quieter. The monkeys were desperate from lack of sleep. "We shall go mad!" they whimpered.

As the sun dipped into the sea, bit by bit the singing faded. The exhausted animals shut their eyes and fell asleep. And as the last voice died away, the monkeys too were finally able to sleep.

Such a hush and stillness fell over the island that you might have wondered if anything lived there at all. But there was still one remaining noise – a bubbly, piping sound from the island's damp places. It was the frogs. No one had told them about the concert, they had been asleep all day, too deep in the mud to have heard anything, and they were now just waking up.

But it was not an unpleasant noise and the other animals were too tired to be annoyed. One thing was certain: they could not spend another whole day singing, just so the frogs would sleep at night. Once was quite enough.

All the animals, including the monkeys, slept right through the night. And when the sun rose, they all awoke. Except the frogs of course, they were just falling asleep!

And that's the way it has been ever since.

❧

Wild Pig blushed – somebody had asked Tortoise for the story of Brave Pig.

"Do you mind if I tell it?" asked Tortoise kindly.

Pig shrugged, he didn't really mind; after all, it had happened a long time ago.

So Tortoise told the story…

❧

Once, long ago, Wild Pig had been a bully. He was a mean, spiteful, self-satisfied show-off. He thundered through the ferns and grasses of the island's forest frightening the jungle-fowl and chipmunks out of their skins. He would only laugh at the flurry of feathers and their terrified squeaks. Pig, after all, was afraid of nothing.

210

The lizards and squirrels, deer and porcupine, all disliked this particular wild pig. They could never curl up safely in a patch of sunlight on the mossy forest floor, for it was quite likely that Pig, with a snort and delighted squeal, would come galloping through the undergrowth and leap right over them – or, more often, leap not quite far enough and land right on top of them. Pig's hooves were hard and his tusks very sharp.

He never seemed able to apologise for his clumsiness. By night or day, scaring the island animals out of their wits seemed to him to be one huge joke. According to Pig, no one was as fearless and intelligent as himself; no one could run round the island quicker; no one was quite as sensible, agile or handsome as he.

Pig thought he was absolutely perfect.

兎

One dark night, with a broad piggish grin on his snout, Pig woke up one of the shy deer as she slept peacefully in a clearing. He chased her in and out the tree trunks, slashing at the ivy and creeper with his tusks, this way and that, squealing as only a wild pig can.

"Afraid, eh?" he cried with a laugh. "Coward! Coward!"

To the deer he seemed like a bad dream come to life. Quail and Pheasant comforted the little deer when at last she stopped running in circles. Her black nose twitched and her dainty legs quivered in fear.

"If only there was a way we could show Pig up, in front of all the other animals on the island," said Quail, "if we could just make him see what it's like to be made a fool of."

"What we need to do is to frighten Pig," said

Pheasant.

So, bobbing and pecking on the forest floor, they hatched a plan.

❧

Quail did not roost at sunset that evening. When it was dark she went to a clearing in the forest where she knew the glow-worms gathered.

"I badly need your help," she said to them, as the little beetles moved among the leaves, their tails glowing bright green, "we are all being terrorised by Wild Pig."

But the glow-worms didn't seem very interested in her plan. Quail became quite severe. "Normally," she said, "we jungle fowl are asleep by now, so we don't have the opportunity to eat you glow-worms. But, if that were somehow to change... and staying up late became an unfortunate habit..."

"We'll help," said the glow-worms, quickly. "We're ready when you give the call."

Pheasant, meanwhile, had been to see one of the monkeys; they were known to be clever with their hands. Monkey thought Pheasant's plan a good joke and he also agreed to help.

Finally, Quail talked with the young deer who had been badly treated by Pig and asked her if she was brave enough to lure Pig down to the big rock by the drinking pool.

"Flatter him," said Quail. "Say how brave and strong he is; ask him to escort you to the pool because you are thirsty – yet afraid of the dark and of monsters and dream-beasts that may lurk in the shadows. He is so vain he will be unable to refuse you."

The young deer said yes, she too would help in curing Pig of his nastiness.

The next afternoon, on the slope of the big rock by the drinking pool, Monkey painted an enormous face; a face with jagged teeth and horrible eyes. No one could see the face because Monkey had drawn it with a pointed stick dipped in wild honey, but the glow-worms would easily be able to find the sweet sticky lines of the drawing.

Now every part of Quail's plan was ready.

That night there was no moon. It was very dark. "Good luck, everyone," clucked Quail.

The young deer looked for Pig. He was easy to find, snorting and grunting as he nosed the ground in search of tender roots.

"What do *you* want?" he asked gruffly when he saw the deer.

"Oh, brave handsome Pig," said Deer meekly, "I need your help. It's a hot night and I'm thirsty, but it's so dark that I'm quite lost and unable to find my way to the drinking pool."

"Well, you'll have to stay thirsty," said Pig rudely. "I'm busy."

"I only asked," Deer went on, "because your courage is well known to all of us. You are strong and wise and scared of nothing."

"That may well be true," said Pig, looking up for a moment, "but a pig has to eat. I told you, I'm busy. Go away."

"You see," said Deer, not giving up yet, "I have asked everyone else to lead me to the pool and no one will help. The forest is too dark tonight and they are afraid of what terrible unknown things might lie in wait."

"A lot of nonsense!" snuffled Pig.

"Oh, if only I was as brave as you!" sighed Deer.

"Just a hoof-load of old stories," said Pig, "invented in order to keep youngsters at home."

"Oh, Pig," said Deer, "if only I could convince myself of that. Of course," she added, "the others did say that even you would refuse. On a night as black as this, they all said, even Pig will feel a little afraid and stay in his lair and tell you to leave him in peace until morning."

"Oh," snorted Pig, thoughtfully, "they said that?"

"Yes," sighed Deer, in mock despair, "and I suppose they were right; it was just too much to ask after all; one couldn't expect it, even of the bravest Pig."

Deer began to wander away into the shadows.

"Wait a moment," grunted Pig, "you are obviously such a nervous weakling that I've decided to change my mind. Follow me."

So Pig set off, his snout searching out the scented forest trails that led to the drinking pool. As Deer followed, she noticed Pig seemed slightly on edge. Sometimes he would stop and listen. "What's that?" he'd ask; the merest rustle of leaves or flutter of moths made him jump.

"Oh, Pig," whispered Deer, "I am so afraid."

"No need," snuffled Pig, "no need." But he didn't sound very sure of himself.

"Are you certain that there are no such things as monsters of the night?" asked Deer, as she followed him.

"Of course," Pig replied, his tusks chattering a little. "Of course I'm sure."

They came into the clearing by the drinking pool. All was quiet except for the gurgling of the spring at the foot of the smooth rock face; except for the 'cluck' from a quail roosting somewhere in the Rizzleberry tree. Pig himself felt rather uneasy; he was secretly glad that Deer was there with him.

That quiet call from Quail had been a signal to the waiting glow-worms: they had already taken up their positions on the lines of honey drawn by Monkey; the whole of the rock-face was thick with them. On hearing Quail's signal, all together they lit their tails.

There, out of the blackness, towering above Pig and Deer, a huge and hideous green face appeared!

Pig's scream echoed round and round the island. Everyone heard it. He was off, crashing blindly through the undergrowth, tripping and skidding, his little hooves carrying him away from the terrible glowing beast faster than he had ever been before.

Many of the animals who had hidden in the bushes around the drinking pool began cheering and laughing: what a sight it had been, Brave Pig in a panic! He would never live it down.

Tortoise had found Pig the next morning, cowering miserably in his lair. Although Pig knew it had all been a tease, his teeth still chattered. What disgrace he felt.

"Never mind," said Tortoise, "cheer up. I'm sure that if you can forgive us, then we can all forgive you."

Pig had looked up then, with a glimmer of hope in his moist eyes. "I am going to change," he said.

And he did.

❧

Tortoise had come to the end of his story.

"You can all see," said Pig, rather embarrassed, "that although I'm still a bit clumsy, I am nevertheless a completely new and likeable animal – considerate, brave, modest; improving all the time."

Tortoise smiled. "Dear Pig," he said, "I don't know what we would do without you."

❧

Tortoise loved the moon, and he loved the sea. On moonlit nights the foam washing in on the edge of the waves seemed as white and rounded as snow.

On just such a night, when the animals had followed Tortoise down to the beach, one of the chipmunks was reminded of his favourite story: "Tell us about snow, Tortoise," he squeaked, "please tell us."

It had only snowed once on Firefly Island, as far as anyone could remember; as far as Tortoise could remember anyway – and wasn't he the oldest and wisest of them all?

So Tortoise settled down in the damp sand and told them the story of the snow...

∽

In a burrow under the toadleaf tree there once lived a fat chipmunk. This chipmunk didn't join in the great games of chase and tag that were carried on by the squirrels in the lower branches of the trees. Nor did she seem to want to play hide-and-seek in and out the boulders and burrows of the forest floor.

The truth was she felt shy, and could never find enough courage to join in. And because she didn't *ask* to play, the others thought she didn't *want* to play – so they never bothered about her. She ended up being left out of everything. "Hi, Sleepyhead!" was the most anyone ever said to her.

Leading a solitary life was very boring. She had nothing to do all day long but follow her instinct for collecting and hoarding. Soft berries and fungi she couldn't resist eating on the spot, and that was why she grew fat, but dry nuts and seeds she stored in the trunk of a huge dead tree that stood at the foot of the mountain. At the bottom of this trunk was a hole hidden by a stone. Much higher up was another hole, and this was where she poked the nuts and seeds she had collected in her dry mouth pouches.

Since there was always food of one sort or another available on the island, such an enormous store was quite pointless. But filling it occupied her lonely days; growing fatter and fatter, she ate and collected and slept, every day was the same.

When the other squirrels grew tired of playing, which wasn't often, they too would idly store away a bit of food. But their hoards were usually in damp or obvious places: the mice and crows would raid them or sometimes Pig or Porcupine would stumble upon them and that would be that. More often than not the squirrels simply forgot where their stores were hidden, and the nuts and seeds rotted or sprouted when the rains came.

※

One day, during the cool season, the unsettled weather grew more than usually cool – it grew very cold indeed. The sky over the sea became heavier and greyer by the hour. The finches perched silent in the trees, as if they had some foreboding of disaster.

The cutting wind came first, from the shadow side of the island. The leaves spun, showing their silver undersides. "It's going to rain," said Pig, knowingly; the cold penetrated his bristly fur. He shivered.

The wind increased in strength, the tree tops heaved; fruit and berries fell to the forest floor: *tump*, *tump* they went as they hit the ground. The squirrels came in from their playing and huddled together underground. How the wind seemed to search and search down their long burrow tunnels.

The gale blew the nuts from the trees and bushes; they fell like hailstones, *putt*, *putt*, *putt* against the leaves. Porcupine huddled in his tiny cave; the deer sheltered behind the rocks by the drinking pool, and the air was filled with wind-tossed blossom.

But it wasn't blossom time! These petals were snowflakes, and now the deer had cold white noses.

Already littered with nuts and berries blown from the trees, the forest floor filled up with snow. Deeper it grew, so that the squirrels' burrows became muffled and dark. And still it snowed. And still the icy wind blew.

"What is it?" said the animals. "What has happened?"

The wind blew all that night. The snow heaped up in drifts around the tree trunks. Even if the squirrels had remembered where their stores lay hidden they could not have got at them.

At first light everyone was cold and hungry. The wind had dropped but the sky hung heavy and grey and the forest lay deep in snow. The branches were bare of food. The monkeys were hungry, the deer were hungry, the mice and finches were hungry. Pig was hungry.

"We're going to die, aren't we?" said Hedgehog to Tortoise. Tortoise felt too cold and slow to answer. He stared out over the endless sea. But it was true, for if the small animals and birds didn't get any food soon they would probably die – some of them that very day.

The squirrels tunnelled desperately in and out of the snow looking for their hidden supplies. They blamed wild pigs and crows for stealing them.

The fat and lonely chipmunk woke cold and hungry like everyone else. Hedgehog's snout came snuffling at her burrow entrance hoping for a snail or worm.

"Good morning," said Hedgehog, "you've missed out on everything as usual."

He told Chipmunk all about the storm and how the cold blossom-like snow now covered everything; he told her how the birds and animals would soon starve to death one by one, beginning with the smallest, which meant mice and squirrels like her. "If you don't believe me, come and see the snow for yourself," said Hedgehog.

Chipmunk, barely awake, followed Hedgehog out of her burrow. It certainly was cold. The snow beneath her paws woke Chipmunk up. "There's no need..." she muttered to herself.

"There's no need... what?" asked Hedgehog.

"There's no need to starve," said Chipmunk, suddenly bright-eyed. Then she told Hedgehog why.

Hedgehog grew very excited. "Come on," he fussed, "what are we waiting for! Let's go and find this tree of yours."

As they set out for the dead tree at the foot of the mountain, Hedgehog told everyone about Chipmunk's secret store.

"If this is a joke, then it's a very cruel one," said the other squirrels. But they followed her all the same for anything was worth trying.

Soon there was a fluttering and hopping procession of birds and small animals going towards the edge of the forest. Tortoise and Pig had helped to flatten some sort of a path through the deep snow. It wasn't long before they had all gathered at the foot of the tall bleached tree that stood among a jumble of boulders at the bottom of the mountain.

At first Chipmunk couldn't find the stone that blocked the lower hole of her food store. The others helped to clear away the snow. When at last they found it, the stone wouldn't move. Pig swung at it with his tusks; the whole clearing held its breath.

And then the stone spun aside. Out of the hole

spurted a wave, a flood, an avalanche of dry nuts, golden seeds and hard-skinned berries. The foot of the tree swarmed with mice and squirrels, jungle fowl and finches while the larger animals waited their turn. There was plenty for everyone. As quickly as they cleared the food from in front of the hole, more flooded out. There was sufficient dried food stored in the height of that huge hollow tree to keep them all going for many days.

Tortoise wasn't keen on wrinkled berries, but he chewed on them patiently and soon he felt better. Pig stuffed himself with nuts; they were his favourite food.

"We've got a lot to thank you for, Chipmunk," chattered the other squirrels. But, as usual, Chipmunk was barely able to say anything and turned away tied up in knots of shyness.

The snow melted in a few days. The sun shone and the forest dried out. The squirrels went to Chipmunk's burrow every morning and asked her to play. On the fourth day she came outside and watched. On the fifth day she joined in.

༄

It never again snowed heavily on Firefly Island, though sometimes in the cool season the top of the mountain shone crisp and white. The rotten tree eventually blew down, but it was quite empty, for Chipmunk never kept a store again – she was too busy playing. And with all the hiding and chasing she became quite thin and nimble.

"What is it like to be dead?" the squirrels asked Tortoise, when he had finished the story about the snow and everyone almost starving to death.

Tortoise watched the ribbon of waves coming up over the sand. He was not sure. "I look at the fallen leaves and shrivelled mosses," he said, "and I see them ever so slowly become earth. The trees and bushes and plants feed from the earth and we, in turn, feed from them. In this way, the leaves and moss are never lost; they are part of us. How much of me is leaf and moss; how much of me is Tortoise?"

The tide was coming in and frothing around his legs. The squirrels ran further up the beach.

"I cannot see," said Tortoise, puzzled, "exactly where anything begins or ends."

Acknowledgements

The publishers are grateful to the following for permission to include material which is their copyright:

Watson, Little Ltd for *I, Houdini* by Lynne Reid Banks, published by J. M. Dent

David Higham Associates Ltd and the Estate of Roald Dahl for *Esio Trot* by Roald Dahl, published by Jonathan Cape

Curtis Brown Ltd, London on behalf of The University Chest, Oxford, for "The Open Road" from *The Wind in the Willows* by Kenneth Grahame

HarperCollins*Publishers* for *The Magic Pudding* by Norman Lindsay

Aidan Chambers for *Seal Secret* by Aidan Chambers, published by The Bodley Head

A. P. Watt Ltd on behalf of The National Trust for Places of Historic Interest or Beauty for "Tiger Tiger" from *The Jungle Book* by Rudyard Kipling

Alexandra Cann on behalf of Colin Dann for *Farthing Wood, the Adventure Begins*, published by Hutchinson

A. P. Watt Ltd on behalf of Foxbusters Ltd for *The Crowstarver* by Dick King-Smith, published by Transworld Ltd

Ben Blathwayt for *Stories from Firefly Island* by Ben Blathwayt, published by Julia MacRae